AWAKENING MRS LORD

A SAPPHIC AGE GAP ROMANCE IN THE 1940S

AVEN BLAIR

CONTENTS

Copyright Page

ALSO BY AVEN BLAIR

CHAPTER 1

NORA

Leaving Savannah Georgia
December 27, 1947

As Anna and I prepare to leave her Mother's home in Savannah, a sharp ache fills my heart, and I fight the urge to cry. "Wait!" I blurt out instinctively. Anna slams on the brakes, her eyes wide with panic as she turns to me.

"What's wrong?!" she asks in a frantic tone. Looking at her, my mind races with reasons to go back inside her Mother's house before we leave.

"I'll be right back; I think I forgot something in my room," I say as I exit the car. Making my way inside the home, I'm immediately met by Vanessa, Anna's Mother.

"Nora?" She says in her warm, soothing tone.

"Hi, um, I think I forgot something in my room," I mumble, heading toward the bedroom where I've spent the past week during Christmas. But then I pause, turning back to see Vanessa watching me. Her gaze softens, and a familiar sparkle lights her eyes. Slowly, I walk toward her, my heart pounding. As I slip into her arms, I whisper, "I didn't forget anything except to tell you what a wonderful woman you are."

Vanessa pulls me close and whispers, "Thank you, Nora." She holds me tightly and adds, "I hate that you have to leave."

"Me too. I don't want to leave you," I reply, fighting back tears. As I release Vanessa, our eyes catch, and I ask softly, "May I telephone you when I get home?" Vanessa touches my cheek and kisses it.

She walks over to the kitchen desk, scribbles something, and carefully folds the paper. Returning to me, she slips it into my jacket pocket, leaning in close. Her voice is soft as she says, "Yes, Nora. I would like it very much if you telephoned me."

Suddenly, Anna honks the horn, and we both smile and chuckle. "Well, I better go; Anna's ready to return to Birmingham." Vanessa nods, her soft brown eyes meeting mine, the same eyes I've been lost in all week. I pull her into a tight hug, pressing a kiss to her cheek, and then, before I fall apart, I turn and walk away.

I jump into Anna's car, and she quickly asks, "What did you leave?"

"Nothing. It must be in my suitcase," I reply, turning my head away from her.

"Are you okay?" She asks.

Not wanting Anna to know why I'm upset or went back inside her Mother's home, I quickly say, "Yeah, but I don't feel well. I'm feeling nauseous all of a sudden." It's not exactly a lie —I do feel sick like I could almost throw up.

"Well, let me know if I need to pull over," Anna says. I just nod, then stare out the car window as the ache in my heart tightens. The farther we drive from Savannah—from Vanessa, the worse it gets. This awful knot in my heart grips me tighter with every passing mile.

Suddenly, I shout, "Pull over."

As soon as I exit the car, I double over, vomiting and crying uncontrollably. The aching is unbearable, and the worst part is hiding the real reason from Anna. I glance southeast, longing to run back—to her, back into Vanessa's arms—but I know that's impossible. I pull a handkerchief from my jacket pocket, wiping my face and forcing myself to breathe to pull it together. Then I climb back into the car.

"What made you so sick, Nora?" Anna asks with a puzzled look on her face.

"I don't know, it just hit me all at once," I say, staring straight ahead, unable to look at her.

"I'm going to pull over and get you a soda. Grab your pillow from the trunk and lie in the back seat. Okay?"

"Thank you," I tell her, then nod, gazing straight ahead.

As I lie in the back seat, the silence between Anna and me feels heavier with each passing mile. She hasn't said much to me besides asking how I feel, but her frustration with me is clear. I know she was upset several times during the visit, and I can't blame her. Instead of going out with her and her friends, I stayed at her mom's house, choosing to remain close to Vanessa. I was drawn to her in a way I couldn't explain, even to myself.

Knowing I need to talk with Anna, I say, "Thank you for the soda, it helped. I'm feeling better."

She simply nods and replies, "Good."

Sitting up, I lean against the front seat, gazing out the windshield. "Anna, I'm sorry I upset you and didn't go out with you and your friends."

Anna shakes her head and replies, "Well, there is no need to argue about it now. I just don't understand why you chose to stay with Mother so much," She says exasperatedly.

I quickly reply, "Because your Mom is nice and she and I

have much in common, both artists. Besides, she isn't *old*, Anna."

"It just felt weird you being there instead of with me and friends closer to our age," she says tartly. Then adds, "I love Mother, but I know why Dad left her."

"And why is that, Anna?" I ask politely, not wanting to anger her.

"Because she's just been a recluse for too long. After she sold her business four years ago, all she wants to do is stay locked up in her damn workspace and paint," Anna growls.

Softly, I ask, "What's wrong with that? I'd love to have a space like that for my photography instead of my one-bedroom apartment." Leaning my chin on my arms resting on the front seat, I add, "I thought he left because he found someone else."

"He did!" she snaps, then adds, "I don't care for her, but at least she isn't a recluse like Mother." I don't like Anna's tone, but I choose not to defend Vanessa right now. That would only create more strife between us, so I let it go.

This awful ache in my heart is still very much there, but I know I need to mend things with Anna. "I feel better and can drive whenever you get tired."

"I'm fine," she replies quickly. I lie back down, knowing she's still mad at me, and turn over meeting this terrible ache. How did I let myself fall for Vanessa, and why? As the tears reemerge, I realize it just happened during our time together. How could I not fall for that enchanting woman whose soft brown eyes and smile rendered me completely lost?

Reaching into my pocket, I feel the slip of paper she tucked in before I left. I want to read it so badly, but not near Anna. It seems like she wrote more than just her phone number because she scribbled for much longer than it would have taken to write a simple number. I'll have to wait until I get to my apartment; reading anything she wrote would most likely send me spiraling.

It's late-afternoon, and Anna just dropped me off at my apartment. We hugged goodbye, and she was more cordial with me than on the drive back.

Entering my apartment, I drop my luggage, walk over to the sofa, and collapse onto it, thinking of Vanessa. Her warm brown eyes seemed to love me from the moment we met. Though I know it's in her nature to be kind, there's something more in the way she gazed at me. As I start crying again, I realize how much I miss her smile and being close to her. Photographing her while she painted felt so intimate as I watched her through my viewfinder.

Sitting up, I reach into my pocket and pull out the note she had tenderly folded before slipping it into my jacket, gazing into my eyes, and giving me a warm smile. Opening it, I read:

Nora,
Please telephone me when you're
home—I would love nothing more than to hear
your voice and feel close to you again.
~Vanessa
AD-3062

With a wide grin, I place the note to my face and inhale deeply, catching her subtle scent. My heart aches for her, and I can't help but wonder how she truly feels about me. As I reread the note, I know the last four words—*feel close to you again*—must mean something significant.

Lying back against the sofa, I close my eyes and replay the intimate moments Vanessa and I shared in her art workspace. Once, as I was photographing her, she paused, looked at me warmly, and said, 'You're a beautiful woman, Nora. I hope you know how special you are.' Then, a tender smile lingered on her lips for a while before she returned to her painting.

After her remark, I could no longer shoot, so I settled onto the small sofa in her workspace, lay against the armrest, and gazed at her. My eyes traveled over every part of her, memorizing every inch of her mature beauty. Vanessa noticed me watching her, our eyes locked, and she offered me a tender smile, winking before resuming her work.

That night, as I lay in bed, I gave myself orgasm after orgasm, lost in fantasies of making love to her.

Vanessa's scent lingers on my clothing, a reminder of her warm embrace before we parted one another this morning, bringing tears to my eyes once more. This love feels impossible—because of the distance, our age difference, and especially Anna.

I can't shake the doubt that Vanessa's tenderness toward me might simply be because of my friendship with her daughter. Shaking my head, I think, *No, it's more than that, and I won't let her deny it.*

CHAPTER 2

VANESSA

I'm deeply moved by the sketch I drew of Nora as she lay sleeping against the sofa in my workspace one afternoon after she photographed me. Touching it, I trace all of her delicate and beautiful features, especially her full and sensual lips.

I've wanted to paint Nora since that moment and even before. There is something very special about her; she stirs something in me that no other person ever has. My eyes begin to burn as I gaze at the sketch of her. Putting my fist against my mouth, tears drip, and my heart aches. It shouldn't, but it does.

Walking out of the workroom, I head back into the main house and fix myself a hot cup of tea before settling into the sofa. I pull my legs beneath me and gaze out the front window as I sip my chamomile tea, hoping it will soothe me.

After tea, I walk to my bedroom, lie down on the bed, cover myself, and try to relax. Thoughts of Nora seem to intrude on my every waking moment. Why? She's a young woman, my daughter's friend, and it's unrealistic.

Thinking about her coming back into the house before

she left, her words echo in my mind over and over. *I didn't forget anything except to tell you what a wonderful woman you are.* It makes me smile, but the tears continue to fall.

Remembering the tender moment when I slipped the note with my telephone number into her jacket pocket. Suddenly, I feel a pang of regret—I forgot to ask for hers. Closing my eyes, I force myself to believe she'll call me; why else would she have asked? Yet, I feel completely cut off from her, with no way to reach out. I turn on my side, breathe deeply to calm myself, and hopefully nap for a while.

Waking up, I notice it's dark outside, and the nap I hoped would soothe me has only left me feeling heavy and gloomy. Rising, I head straight to the bathroom and step into the shower, letting the warm water cascade over my body. Thoughts of Nora remain fresh and vivid, but I know I need to will myself to think of something else whenever her lovely face comes to mind. Yet, that's not what I want.

After I dry off, I slip on my blue silk bathrobe and return to the kitchen for another cup of tea. Walking back into the living area, I gaze at the Christmas Tree, still lit up, twinkling and dancing. Smiling, I think about my wonderful time with Anna and Nora here. It's been three years since Anna has spent the holiday with me.

Since our divorce, she has spent most of the holidays with her father. I know she blames me for the breakup between Thomas and me, and she's mostly right. Anna has always been a daddy's girl and chose his side in the divorce. I'm not sure why she sees it as a matter of sides. The truth is, Thomas and I were never truly compatible, and I could never love him the way he wanted. Eventually, he found a woman who could.

Lost in thought, I sit down in my favorite leather Lawson chair. Suddenly, I'm startled by the telephone. Glancing at my wall clock, I see that it's 9 p.m. and wonder who's calling at this hour.

"Hello."

"Hi, Vanessa, it's Nora," she says sweetly.

With a broad grin, I lean forward and close my eyes, picturing her sweet face. "Hi, Nora. Did you make it home okay?" I ask softly.

"Yes, we arrived around 4 o'clock this afternoon," she replies. Then the phone goes silent.

After a moment, I say, "I was hoping you would call me tonight, Nora."

"You were?" she asks surprisingly.

Leaning back, I grin, "Of course, sweetie. I mean, you read my note, didn't you?"

Nora giggles and says, "Yes, I did. It was very sweet. Thank you for the note. You could have just written your number, but I'm glad you wrote more."

"Well, I wanted to make sure you knew that I wanted to hear from you. I enjoyed our time together very much," I tell her tenderly.

In a low tone, Nora replies, "I enjoyed it too."

Realizing that Nora is also struggling with this, I smile and whisper, "I miss you."

Nora clears her throat and softly says, "I miss you too, and I didn't want to leave."

"Nora," I whisper. The phone goes silent again. "Baby, are you okay?"

I hear her quiet tears, and she faintly says, "No, not really. Vanessa. I have to hang up before saying things I probably shouldn't." Then the line goes dead. Placing the receiver back on the cradle, I break down and weep. I'm weeping for Nora more than I am for myself. I don't think either of us realized what has happened to us until now.

With three hundred miles separating us, the pain is almost intolerable, and I can't let her stay in this pain alone. Picking up the receiver, I call the operator and ask for the number that just called me. Dialing it, I try to calm myself, knowing I must be gentle yet strong for her.

"Hello," she says quietly.

"Nora, sweetheart, don't hang up again, I can do most of the talking if you'd like."

"I'm sorry, Vanessa."

"You don't have anything to be sorry about, Nora. Obviously, we both care deeply for one another, and I want to continue talking with you, whether you're here in my home or three hundred miles away. Okay?"

Nora softly chuckles and says, "Okay, and yes, I want to continue talking with you as well. The drive home was just dreadful."

"Why, Nora?" I ask gently.

"Because every mile I traveled away from you felt like one hundred, and Anna was upset with me, so the ride home was mostly silent and painful," she says as she cries.

"I'm sorry, Nora. Is she upset because you and I spent so much time together?"

"Yes. I know I should have gone out with her and her friends, as she reminded me on the drive home, but I just didn't want to."

With a light chuckle, I say, "That makes two of us." Nora laughs—a bright sound that instantly makes me smile. I can picture that laugh just as vividly as I saw it all last week. Then I add, "Nora, after you get a good night's sleep, you'll feel better. You're just emotionally tired and need to rest."

"Yeah, you're right, I'm definitely emotional," she says with a soft laugh.

"I know, love. Why don't you take a warm bath or shower and then go to bed? I promise you will feel one hundred percent better in the morning."

Nora is silent for a moment, then replies, "You're right. I'll feel better, but not one hundred percent."

Pondering her statement, I tenderly say, "You will in a few days, love."

"No, I don't think so, Vanessa, but it's sweet of you to comfort me," she replies. Closing my eyes, I wish more than anything that I could pull her through the phone line into my arms.

"Nora, would it be better if we didn't talk?" I ask gently.

"God, no! I couldn't take that," she replies in an upset tone.

"Okay, love. Neither could I," I say softly. Then I add, "Nora, I have your number now. May I call you tomorrow night?"

"Yes, please," she murmurs. "I could talk with you every day."

Smiling, I say, "So could I, but not if it makes you this sad."

"Does it make you sad, Vanessa?" she asks. Taking a deep breath, I know the real question she's asking, so I hesitate for a moment.

"Vanessa?" she whispers.

With an open heart, I confess, "Nora, yes, it does, and I miss you dreadfully." Then I begin to weep. I try to stop, but my feelings for her are so raw—yet beautifully painful.

"Oh god," she whispers as she softly cries. After a moment, she says my name sweetly, "Vanessa?"

"Yes, love?" I reply. Then she's silent again. I wait on her for a moment, then add, "Nora, say what you need to."

"May I come back to you tomorrow?" she asks, her voice barely above a whisper.

My head screams no, but my heart beats for her. "Nora," I whisper, my mind racing with how we ended up here. We spent the entire week together, sharing countless tender and sometimes flirtatious moments. Yet, neither of us truly understood what we felt until this expansive distance severed us, leaving us yearning for one another more than we ever could have imagined.

After a moment, I whisper, "Yes." Then I ask, "What about work?"

She immediately replies, "I have a wedding to photograph in two weeks, and my other commitments aren't until after the first of the year."

"Nora, we need to think about this, love."

"I know, Vanessa. I realize everything has changed, and I know what I want when I come to you. Is it what you want?" she asks confidently. Closing my eyes, I realize what she is asking, and now I have to decide if I am ready. Can I let another woman in? Most importantly, do I want to lose her?

Opening my eyes, I gaze at the twinkling of Christmas tree lights and see her laughing. Without hesitation, I say, "Yes, Nora, this is what I want, but we must take things slowly."

"Vanessa," she whispers sweetly. "I thought you would say no, thank god you didn't."

"How could I say no to you, Nora? But I will only let you come under one condition."

"Okay?" she asks hesitantly.

"I'll pay for your train ticket," I say sternly. Nora laughs, and I hear the beautiful melody that filled my home during Christmas.

"So if I say no, I can't come," she asks playfully.

"Correct!" I say with a chuckle.

"Then I guess I'll be forced to accept your kind generosity, ma'am," she says as her playful charm emerges—the same charm that won my heart as soon as she stepped into my home a week ago.

With laughter, I say, "Listen, darling, I want you to take that bath and then go to bed. Okay?"

"Your tenderness for me is almost overwhelming, Vanessa."

"Well, I care deeply for you, Nora," I tell her sweetly. The line falls silent again, but we linger in the stillness, suspended by our devotion to one another.

CHAPTER 3

NORA

"I care deeply for you, too, Vanessa," I reply softly. Then I smile, pulling my legs against my chest as I sit on my sofa in the stillness of our tenderness.

After a moment, Vanessa softly says, "Nora, the train most likely leaves very early, so you need to rest. You've had an exhausting day, so you must go to bed. Okay?""Yes, you're right, I do. I suppose I should say goodnight then."

"Thank you, Nora. It's been a long time since someone made me feel this way and this special."

"Well, that's a damn shame because, as I told you this morning, you are indeed a wonderful woman, Vanessa Lord."

With a soft chuckle, Vanessa says, "Get some sleep, love, and I'll pick you up at the train station tomorrow."

"Goodnight, Vanessa."

"Sweet dreams, my lovely Nora," she says with her low, soothing voice.

Birmingham Union Station

Sunday

Boarding *the Southern Railway*, I settle into my first-class seat. Vanessa called early this morning to let me know she'd purchased my ticket and that it was waiting for me.

As I sink into the plush seat, I smile, gazing out the vast window, knowing that I'll be with her again within a few hours, enveloped in our shared solitude. The train jolts forward, and a wave of anxiousness stirs within me, much like the nerves that crept in during our phone call last night.

Watching the Liberty Statue glide past atop the Liberty National Building, I suddenly feel very alive. As the train picks up speed, my mind drifts back in time to Carol and the two years we spent together in college. She was the first woman I ever made love to, the first I ever loved, but she broke my heart. Since then, I've dated here and there, but the idea of finding love again has felt so distant, too exhausting, and too dangerous. It's hard to constantly hide who I am. After Carol, nothing seemed worthwhile anymore.

Glancing at my watch, I notice it's almost 3 p.m. We should be nearing the *Central of Georgia Railway Passenger Station*. Suddenly, anxiety grips me, but I know that once I see Vanessa, her calming presence will wash over me like the warmth of the morning sun.

I hold out my hands and see they're trembling. Clasping them together, I smile, greeting Savannah, the beautiful city I left only yesterday. With a smile, I think: It *would have been easier if I had just stayed in Savannah.*

As the train slowly pulls into the station, I spot her immediately. She's waiting for me, and I can't take my eyes off her. She's so gorgeous, with her dark shoulder-length hair and her body wrapped elegantly in a gray wrap-coat tied at the waist, showing her lovely silhouette.

Vanessa glances up, and our eyes lock. She doesn't smile

but gives me a look unlike any she gave me last week. My heart surges and shudders, and I freeze, taking in her quiet confidence and maturity.

I'm not a girl—I'm a twenty-nine-year-old woman. Yet no one has ever looked at me this way before. In this moment, she moves me sensually and seduces me all at once, our eyes refusing to break. I touch the glass, my fingers trembling, and she winks tenderly before her lips curve into a sweet, knowing smile. She's releasing me to come to her.

As I disembark, I walk straight into her arms. Neither of us speaks. Vanessa holds me close, instinctively knowing what I need. In a soft whisper, she says, "I'm so happy you're here, Nora. It's only been one day, but it felt like forever."

"I know, it was awful," I reply. After a moment in her arms, I reluctantly pull away and say, "I should get my luggage." Vanessa smiles, wraps her arm around me, and gives a soft chuckle as we walk toward baggage claim together.

With a soft laugh I say, "I haven't even unpacked yet!" Vanessa laughs louder, threading her fingers through my hair, sending delightful chills through every nerve in my body. My God, I think to myself: *this is a completely different woman than the one I left just yesterday.*

After the porter places my luggage in the trunk, Vanessa walks to the passenger door and opens it for me, her eyes never leaving mine. My entire body buzzes with anticipation as I meet her gaze. "Thank you, Miss Lord," I say with a playful giggle.

"You're welcome, Nora," she replies, her voice rich with affection as her eyes linger on mine.

After Vanessa gets into the car, she turns toward me. Instinctively, our fingers intertwine, and she gives me a tender smile and then asks, "How was your train ride?"

Shyly, I look away, then glance back into her lovely eyes

and say, "It was good. Thank you for the first-class ticket. It wasn't necessary, but it was very thoughtful."

Vanessa reaches toward me, tucks a few strands of hair behind my ear, and then softly says, "Well, I happen to think it was necessary."

Smiling at me, she asks, "Are you hungry?" I shake my head no. She winks as she releases my hand, starts the Buick, and then drives us toward her home. Glancing out the window, I can't help but notice that the awful ache in my heart has dissipated and has been replaced with a soothing warmth.

Walking into Vanessa's house immediately makes me feel like I'm home again. Sitting my luggage down in the entry-way, I look at her and ask, "Should I put my suitcase back in my room?" Then I shake my head and smile at her.

Vanessa walks to me, reaches for the scarf that she gave me for Christmas, grasps each side of it, and says, "This scarf is so beautiful on you, Nora."

Meeting her brown eyes, I hold them and say, "I love it, Vanessa. It's the most beautiful scarf I've ever had." I glance away and lightly chuckle, then add, "I have a confession."

Vanessa gives me a sweet, quizzical look and softly asks, "Please tell me, Nora."

Gazing into her eyes with newfound confidence, I confess, "I slept with it wrapped around me last night." Vanessa's expression shifts from tender to serious in an instant. She glances at my lips, then back into my eyes.

Then she pulls me close, and I wrap my arms around her neck, feeling like I never want to be anywhere else but in her embrace. She whispers, "That makes me happy, Nora." This intense moment feels magical. I close my eyes, wanting to see nothing, only to feel her body pressed against mine.

Releasing me slowly, she looks at me and says, "Go put your things up, and I'll make us some tea." I smile and nod, then walk back to my room. Walking back into the room I stayed in last week feels odd. This time there is no agenda, no expectations, and thankfully no Anna.

Finding my way to the kitchen, I see Vanessa pouring hot water into our teacups. I walk over and lean against the counter. She glances at me, smiles, and chuckles, and I giggle along with her before saying, 'I'm glad you wanted me to come back."

As she dances the tea bags in the hot water, she softly says, "I never wanted you to leave, Nora." My whole feminine core buzzes, and my heart beats with tender pain. Vanessa turns her head toward me, smiles, and then hands me my teacup. "Let's go into the living room, love."

As I walk toward the loveseat with my tea, Vanessa says, "Nora, please sit with me on the sofa." Nodding, I meet her eyes and smile.

Sipping my tea, I feel my anxiety resurface, almost gripping me. Vanessa must sense it because she sets her teacup on the side table and moves closer, placing her arm around the back of the sofa. "Nora, please don't be nervous, love. You and I had such an amazing week together. I know things are different now, but I'm still the same."

"No… no, you're not, Vanessa, and neither am I," I say hesitantly as I sip my tea. She threads her fingers gently through my hair. I close my eyes and whisper, "See, you never did this once last week. Everything has changed."

Opening my eyes, I meet her gaze. "Maybe I didn't, Nora, but I certainly wanted to," she says, stroking my hair with tenderness. As she does, I wonder where my confidence has gone; it simply waxes and wanes in her presence.

CHAPTER 4

VANESSA

Stroking Nora's soft blonde hair through my fingers brings up feelings I've repressed for so long. Releasing her soft hair from my fingertips, I reach for my tea and begin sipping it as I stay close to Nora. Gazing at her, I say, "Nora, I was thinking about something."

Setting her cup on its saucer, Nora turns toward me and asks, "What are you thinking?"

Smiling at her, I reply, "Well, I woke during the night, and my thoughts immediately found you." Nora grins at me and then takes another sip of tea. Then I add, "How would you feel about us taking a trip together tomorrow morning to *Blowing Rock*, North Carolina?"

Nora's eyes flash with excitement that warms me. "Wow, I don't know what to say. I mean, what about your painting?"

Laughing, I say, "Despite what Anna may say about me, I am not a complete recluse."

"I'm sorry, Vanessa, I didn't mean that."

"I know you didn't. Nora, over the last few years, I've chosen to live a secluded, simple life to get in touch with myself and remember who Vanessa is."

Nora sets her teacup on the side table, then shifts her body toward me. With a soft, serious gaze, she sweetly asks, "Did you find her?"

Touching her cheek, I see her earnest and sincere concern. Nodding, I smile and say, "Yes, I found her, and I actually like her a lot."

Giving me a wide grin, Nora says, "I like her too." Then she threads her fingers through my hair. I close my eyes, and all the feelings from years ago come crashing through me. I quickly think of Jinny and her love for me, but that was so long ago; it was a different time.

Opening my eyes, I see this young, gorgeous woman who obviously wants to be near me, and she makes me incredibly happy. I reach up and touch her hand as it travels through my hair, close my eyes again, and surrender to my feelings for Nora.

With my eyes closed I hear her softly say, "A trip with you would be lovely, Vanessa." Opening my eyes, I smile at her and nod.

"I want us to leave in the morning, Nora. You're probably traveled out, sweetheart, but I'll drive, and you can sleep in the back if you'd like. Would that be okay?"

Nora smiles brightly. "Yes, I'd love to leave in the morning. We should go to your workspace right now and pack your supplies because I know you'll want to paint the Blue Ridge Mountains. I can't wait to photograph them."

She stands and reaches out for my hand. Taking her soft hand, I stand beside her and smile into her blue-green eyes. "Have you ever seen the color of the water at the Emerald Coast?" I ask softly. She nods and smiles. "It's the color of your lovely eyes, Nora."

"Thank you, Vanessa," she says, then grins at me for a moment before tugging at my hand. "Come on, let's go pack your art supplies."

CHAPTER 4

Nora gently releases my hand as we enter my workspace and walks to my painting area, where the large canvas I've been working on since yesterday stands. She approaches it, places her hands to her face, and gazes at the portrait I'm painting of her. I walk up behind her and wrap my arms around her. I shouldn't, but I can't help myself. "Do you like it, Nora?" I whisper against her ear.

Feeling her nod, I smile, inhaling her sweet scent that enchanted me the entire week of Christmas. "I remember this moment, Vanessa," she says softly.

"What do you remember about it?" I ask.

She pauses, then replies, "You looked at me and told me I was beautiful and hoped that I realized how special I was. That moment rendered me unable to shoot anymore. I laid my camera down and kept my eyes on you."

Releasing her, I walk to the painting. "I felt your eyes on me, Nora, and when I glanced back after a while, I saw you sleeping." Turning toward her, I say, "As I sketched you, I knew at that moment what I felt for you."

Nora walks toward me slowly, wrapping her arms around my neck, her body melting into mine. "Oh, Vanessa. You're so lovely."

Holding Nora in my arms here, alone in this sacred workspace that's always been mine, feels intense. Last week, sharing it with her was something special, but now, holding her here in the space I've created is an overwhelming feeling I've never known.

As I continue holding her I say, "I'm going to go cook us dinner; I need to feed you." Nora nods, then squeezes me tighter, and I smile. Releasing her, I catch her hand and say, "Come on, I'll let you help me."

With our fingers intertwined, we quietly walk back to the house; no words are needed. Entering the kitchen, I begin pulling things from the pantry. "I'm going to cook my famous chili. Does that sound good?"

"Yum. Yes, I love chili," Nora says as she smiles into my eyes. Then ask, "What can I do to help?"

"Well, open these cans of tomatoes and beans for me," I say, smiling back at her. As I begin preparing our chili, I can't help but steal glances at her. Nora is such a beauty; I could get used to her very easily—I already have.

Nora begins to laugh and then gives me a surprised look. "What?" I ask.

"We completely forgot to pack your art supplies when we went to your workspace," she says, chuckling.

"I think we got sidetracked," I say, winking at her. Nora looks at me and shyly looks away. "Are you okay?" I ask softly.

As she works on opening the beans, she stops, lays the can opener down, and says, "Yes and no." I gaze at her then she adds, "You completely unnerve me, Vanessa. I should be too embarrassed to admit that, but it's just the damn truth."

Walking to her, I gaze at her and thread my fingers through her soft blonde hair. "It will get easier, Nora. And you obviously don't realize what you do to me, love."

Nora looks into my eyes and asks, "Tell me what I do to you, Vanessa?"

Pulling her to me, I hold her tenderly and say, "I can't put it into words just yet, Nora, but I feel the same things you feel, baby." Nora wraps her arms around my waist and hugs me tightly.

"Good," she says faintly.

"You wouldn't be here in my home, in my arms, had I not fallen for you over the last week," I say as I pull away and look at her. Then I add, "Nora, I adore you, baby. But as I said on the phone, I want us to take things slowly. It's best for both of us, especially you."

Nora nods and says, "Yes, I agree, but saying it is easy, doing it is incredibly hard."

Laughing as I release her, I say, "That is very true." We both chuckle and go back to our tasks. As I think about her question, I am truthful; I can't put it into words just yet. These feelings that I have are so raw but gentle. Nora moves me in ways I haven't felt in years and in many ways ever.

"That chili was amazing, Vanessa. I believe it's the best I've ever eaten, and I've had a lot of chili," she says with a smile. Standing, she takes my bowl along with hers to the kitchen. As I sit at the dining table, I listen to the sounds of a woman in my kitchen, and it makes me smile, but it's a bit frightening as well, especially such a young woman.

All of these conflicting emotions are overwhelming, so I pour myself another glass of wine to help steady my nerves. I've been so concerned with Nora's feelings that I've forgotten to consider my own. My feelings for Nora scare me, but I won't run from them like I did years ago.

Standing, I take our wine glasses and the bottle to the living room. Glancing up, I see Nora walking toward me. She reaches for her glass and takes the wine bottle as well. We sit beside each other on the couch and sip our wine. Nora turns her head toward me and says, "Being back here with you feels wonderful, Vanessa."

Turning to her, I smile and nod, then reach for her hand. Our fingers intertwine, and I begin to stroke her thumb with mine. "Having a woman, and I mean you, Nora, in my home feels right. It may be completely wrong to the outside world, but I no longer live for others," I say, gazing into her blue-green eyes.

"Nora, we will need to be discreet when we travel and stay in *Blowing Rock*, love," I say seriously.

"What concerns you, I mean, besides the obvious?"

"Mainly your… I mean our safety, Nora. Even though you

and I haven't become intimate, others may notice that we care for one another. That concerns me."

"Of course. It does me as well," she says sincerely. Then she looks into my eyes and says, "It's very difficult, Vanessa. I've been with other women, and it's so hard to be discreet. I understand what you're saying."

"You've slept with other women, Nora?" I ask as I gaze at her.

She nods and replies, "Yes, I have. They were kind women, but I've never felt what I feel for you. This is something so beautiful, so ethereal. I can't put it into words either, Vanessa. It's scary, but also very exciting," she says, a softness in her eyes.

"Nora," I whisper. Taking our wine glasses I set them on the side table, take Nora in my arms, and hold her against me as I inhale her scent, "I've smelled you all week, baby."

"Vanessa, the way you hold me is so profound and loving. It's almost hypnotizing."

"You feel amazing in my arms, Nora," I say tenderly as I hold close.

After we finish our wine, I enter my bedroom and begin packing for our trip. Nora went to my workspace to gather the art supplies I asked for. With a light heart, I pack my warm clothing, knowing it will be cold in North Carolina.

Nora enters my bedroom with a glinting smile. She asks, "Do you think it will snow on our trip?" Then she jumps backward onto my bed and laughs.

Seeing the delight in her eyes, I laugh and say, "I sure hope so. Wouldn't that be wonderful?"

"Oh my gosh, yes. It hasn't snowed in Birmingham in a while, and we don't get that much anyway."

"Well, you definitely get more than Savanahians." Nora laughs brightly, the laugh that charmed me Christmas week. Then I ask, "Do you have warm clothing, love? I mean, when you came here, you weren't expecting me to kidnap you and take you two states over."

"I'm not sure if I do, but I'll get by," she says, then looks at me flirtatiously and adds, "I guess you'll be forced to keep me warm, Mrs. Lord." I burst into laughter at her as I shake my head.

"I just unnerved you, didn't I?" She asks with a playful confidence.

As I fold my clothing, I respond, "You did indeed, Miss Wolfe." Then we both laugh.

"Good! I'm glad. I think I just figured out how to unnerve you, so you better watch out, Vanessa Lord," she says, then falls back against my bed and laughs loudly.

As I gaze at her loveliness, I ask playfully, "So you think you have me figured out?" "Oh, hell no!" Nora shouts as she sits back up. "You can never figure out a woman; that is one thing I do know. And I'd never assume I could ever know what goes on in that gorgeous mind of yours, Vanessa." She says with sincere excitement that makes me so happy.

CHAPTER 5

NORA

Vanessa and I packed up and left Savannah at about 8 a.m. We have been traveling for a couple of hours. I turn to her and say, "I don't mind driving if you get tired."

"I'm fine, love. You've traveled enough over the past two days. I'll drive until the afternoon, and then we can find a motel." I continue gazing at her as she smiles, looks at me, and then asks, "What are you thinking, Nora?"

With a smile, I say, "You, of course." She laughs at me and shakes her head. "Actually, I've been thinking of an affectionate name to start calling you. You call me 'Love,' 'Sweetheart,' and when you're especially tender with me, you call me 'Baby.' You've practically used up all the southern endearments on me."

Vanessa laughs loudly and says, "That's because you're too grand for just one term, sweetheart." Then, we both get tickled. "What would you like to call me?" She asks.

Laughing, I say, "I don't know. You choose one for me, okay?"

She looks at me and says, "I don't know; I believe that

should be a term you decide on your own. I'll stick with the three I've already taken, and you can decide what seems fitting."

I look at her with a mischievous grin and ask, "How about, lover."

"Oh dear heavens, Nora, you're going to make me wreck my car." I begin laughing, and then we both get tickled. Vanessa adds, "Maybe later, but not yet, and never in public, love."

"Vanessa, you're such a joy to be with," I say as I continue laughing at her reaction.

After a moment, Vanessa looks serious, so I ask, "What made you so solemn, Vanessa?"

She reaches for my hand, and our fingers intertwine, and then she replies, "Reality, Nora."

"Vanessa, this is reality," I say as I squeeze her hand. "But I understand; are you scared?

"Mostly, I'm not, Nora. I told you I don't live my life for others any longer; however, now my life seems to include you. So that part makes me cautious, baby."

"Vanessa, you do realize I'm a grown woman, right? I'm twenty-nine."

"Of course, but I won't deny that I'm a fifty-year-old woman, which means there's a twenty-one-year age gap between us, which worries me a bit."

"Worries you in what way?" I ask softly

"Oh, Nora, I don't know, love. Perhaps I'm just over-thinking this. I find myself feeling completely protective of you. I admit that you are indeed a grown woman; hell, I've looked at you, and I definitely see a woman, love."

Playfully, I ask, "You've looked at me?"

Vanessa gives me a grin and shakes her head, and says, "You're damn right I've looked at you, Nora."

"Well, Miss Lord, I do believe you're not as tame as I thought you were."

"Tame?" She remarks with a laugh.

Looking straight ahead, I say, "You know damn well what I mean."

After a moment, Vanessa looks at me and replies, "And I believe you're not as innocent as I thought you were, Miss Wolfe."

Glancing quickly at her, I respond, "Innocent?!" Then I chuckle and add, "No, Vanessa, I'm definitely not that."

"Good, I don't want an innocent woman," She replies, then gives me a wink.

It's about 3 o'clock, and Vanessa and I have been traveling for hours. We are enjoying being together again and getting to know one another better. We just found a motel and turned into the parking area. "

Vanessa parks the car, turns toward me, and says, "Well, I'm going to go in and get our rooms, Nora."

Gazing at her, I softly say, "Vanessa, please just get one room. We can have separate beds, but I don't want to sleep away from you tonight."

Vanessa searches my eyes. After a moment, her gaze softens, and she nods, then replies, "Nora, listen... I hate to say this, but two women traveling together and sharing a room might raise some eyebrows. Add an age gap, and people will definitely start talking."

"What are you saying?"

"Nora, we have to think about our safety. The only way you and I can share one room is if we say you're my daughter."

"Your daughter? Oh god, Vanessa," I say with a bit of disgust. Then I glance back at her and see her concern. "You're right. If that is the only way we can share a room, then okay, I'll say I'm your daughter."

"Nora?" She responds a bit sternly.

"Yes? I ask as I turn back to her.

She presses my hand and softly says, "And I mean the whole trip, Nora." Nodding, I look at her, knowing she's right.

"I guess this is reality. Damn, I hate this." I say, looking into her eyes.

"So do I, sweetheart, because that certainly isn't how I see you."

After I think for a minute, I chuckle and say, "Well, It's actually a perfect cover for us. Look at it as a perk for falling for a younger woman."

As Vanessa exits the car, she softly says, "Nora, I already know there are a million perks for falling for you. Being much younger is just one of them, baby. "Then, with a graceful movement, she shuts the door, leaving me staring after her. I watch that incredible woman walk elegantly into the motel office, and with a grin, I realize I'm at a complete loss for words."

Vanessa and I are back in our room after having supper at a local diner. "Thank you for dinner, Vanessa; I enjoyed my meal," I say as I lie on my bed and gaze at her.

"You're welcome, Nora. It was just a simple dinner, but it was good," she replies, smiling at me. Then she asks, "What would you like to do, love?"

"This! Just be with you, Vanessa," I reply with a wink,

which makes Vanessa blush. She laughs, then sits on her bed facing me. Then I add, "I know you're tired; you've been driving all day. You should have let me drive some,"

"You can drive in the morning if you'd like. How about that?"

I simply nod and smile. As I watch Vanessa remove her earrings, she says softly, "I'm glad you're here with me, Nora. Anna's right about me 'locking myself away in my work-space,' but she doesn't understand why. She's young and doesn't see how life can shift under you when you least expect it."

Smiling, I reply, "I know she loves you, Vanessa. But... you're not at all the woman I expected." My gaze softens as I speak.

"I hope that's a good thing," she chuckles, a hint of uncertainty in her voice.

"Vanessa, I'm sharing a motel room with you one week after we met. What does that tell you about what I think of you... or feel for you?"

As she lays her earrings on the side table between us, she smiles and says, "It definitely tells me what I want to hear, Nora."

"Have you and Anna always had a strained relationship?" I ask softly.

"Not when she was young, but things change when girls become teenagers. Thomas and I began to have problems then, and Anna, for some reason, felt she had to choose between us. No matter how much Thomas and I tried to convey that she didn't have to choose a side, she wouldn't hear it."

"That had to be very hard for you, Vanessa?"

Reaching for my hand, she holds it and replies, "It was, baby. But Anna is stubborn like her father. When she has her own children, I hope she will understand that a child needs both parents and choosing between them is harmful."

With a chuckle, I say, "You're right, Anna is definitely stubborn."

Vanessa laughs loudly and nods, "That she is!" Then she stands and opens her suitcase. "I want to take a shower, Nora. If you'd like to go first, I'll wait, love."

While lying on the bed, I reply, "No, you go shower. I'll wait here for you."

"Okay. Don't sneak off somewhere while I'm in there," she says, then gives me a cute smile.

"I'll be right here, lover," Then I laugh loudly as I watch her shake her head at me.

"What am I going to do with you, Nora Wolfe?" She asks playfully as she enters the bathroom.

With a huge grin, I lie back, listen to the shower, and try to visualize the water cascading over that delicious body of hers. My feminine soul pulses with a pulling ache, and I immediately become aroused. "Oh god, how I want that woman," I whisper to myself as my erotic desire for her intensifies.

Hearing the shower stop, I immediately sit up, trying to distract myself. Eyeing the tabletop radio, I stand, walk over, and turn it on. Doris Day's *"It's Magic"* begins to play.

Looking over my shoulder, I see Vanessa stepping out of the bathroom, wrapped in a blue silk robe. Enchanted by her beauty and the song, I gaze at her, and our eyes lock as we hear the words, *"It's magic."*

She walks toward me, never breaking eye contact, and reaches for me. As her head presses gently against mine, we sway, moving slowly in rhythm with the music. My heart races, butterflies fluttering through every nerve in my body.

Vanessa pulls me closer, and I softly kiss her cheek,

inhaling the faint hint of the perfume she clearly applied for me. A smile spreads across my face at the thought. In this enchanting moment, filled with tenderness, I realize with absolute certainty that I'm completely in love with her and want this woman by my side for eternity.

"Thank you, Nora," she whispers as the song fades.

CHAPTER 6

VANESSA

L ying on my side in bed, I face Nora. Gazing at her loveliness, I see her youth. With tenderness, I ask, "Why do you want to be with me, Nora? I'm almost twice your age, baby."

"Vanessa," she whispers softly and remains silent for a moment. Then she adds, "You are the most alluring woman I've ever known. No woman has ever affected me the way you do. It was impossible for me not to fall for you, darling."

Smiling at her, I look into her Emerald Coast eyes and see her love for me. I love her, but I'm sometimes unsure if this is wise. "That's so beautiful, Nora," I reply softly.

"I meant every single one, Vanessa. I have so much more I want to say to you," She replies as she reaches for my hand.

Catching her hand, our fingers intertwine, and I softly say, "My heart is full of words for you, Nora. Please know that I will gladly empty it in time and share everything I hold for you, baby."

"I would love that, Vanessa."

"Goodnight, my lovely Nora."

"Goodnight, darling," she says softly.

As I turn off the lamp between us, I lay in the dark for a moment and tenderly say, "I love the endearing name you've chosen for me, baby."

She giggles and responds, "You are my *darling*, Vanessa."

Smiling, I gaze at her silhouette before closing my eyes, enveloped in a sense of contentment I haven't felt in years. This young woman makes me incredibly happy, and I know I love her. I'm acutely aware of the bumps ahead of us, but on this trip, I only want to live and breathe Nora.

With her beside me, the uncertainties of the future seem distant, overshadowed by the warmth of our connection. I take a deep breath, enjoying the moment, as I let the weight of the world slip away. For now, it's just us, and that's more than enough.

Blowing Rock, North Carolina
The Blue Ridge Inn

"This cabin looks so inviting and charming, Vanessa," Nora says excitedly as we pull up to the lodging we rented for the week.

"Yes, it does, Nora." Looking at the happiness on her sweet face, I smile and then say, "Let's get our luggage, love."

Nora quickly bounces out of her seat and is waiting for me at the back of the car before I ever exit the vehicle. Laughing, I walk back toward her, smiling.

"What's so funny? She asks as she grins.

Shaking my head, I look at my keys to find the one for the trunk. Lifting my eyes to hers with a lift in my voice, I reply, "You, Nora, you make me happy."

Smiling at me, she says, "I want to make you happy forever, Vanessa." My smile turns serious as I gaze at her. My heart falls, and a gentle warmth spreads across my soul at her words.

Putting the key into the truck lock, I pause for a moment, then gaze at her and say, "I want that too, Nora. I want it more than anything."

Nora slips her arm through mine and replies, "Then there is no reason we can't have that, Vanessa. Emotionally seduced by her blue-green eyes, I nod and give her a sweet wink.

Opening the trunk, we grab our suitcases, walk onto the cabin's front porch, and enter it. "Oh, Vanessa. This is lovely," she says with sincere excitement that enchants me.

Walking to the expansive windows that take up the entire wall of one side of the cabin, Nora stops and gazes outward. "This is what I want you to paint for me, Vanessa: *The Blue Ridge Mountains," she* says with conviction.

Walking up behind her, I wrap my arms around her body just as I did that day in my workspace—the day she returned to me. "I'll paint it for you, Nora. I would do anything for you, baby."

"Vanessa," she breathlessly says. "I can't fight this much longer.".

Knowing I can't either, I quickly release her and walk to the fireplace, where the warm fire is already burning. Nora remains where I left her, still gazing out the expansive window. "I'm sorry, baby. I wasn't thinking."

"You don't have to say that, Vanessa. I know what you feel for me and what you need. As I've reminded you, I'm a grown woman. I see the fire in your eyes". She then turns toward me, gives me a seductive look with those piercing blue-green eyes, and adds, "I know exactly what you want, Vanessa."

Breaking our gaze, I look into the fire, nod, and reply, "I know you do, Nora, and I've wanted you all week."

Nora walks to me, stands beside me, catches my hand, and asks, "Are you scared to take me to bed, Vanessa?"

Frightened by her words, I nod and whisper, "Yes." Nora tugs at my hand, then walks us to the couch. We sit beside one another, gazing into the firelight that illuminates the room as it warms us.

Nora interlaces her fingers with mine and then turns toward me. Somehow, in her youthful wisdom, she knows my pain because she gently asks, "A woman broke your heart years ago, didn't she, Vanessa?"

With amazement, I look into her eyes. She sees it in me, the wound from my past. The one I've tried to bury over and over through the years. "How could you possibly know that, Nora?"

"I just know somehow, Vanessa. What was her name?" She asked softly.

Watching the flames from the fire, I whisper, "Jinny." Then I let out a sigh. Pressing her hand against mine, she takes my hand between hers.

"Mine was Carol. I loved her, but after two years together, she couldn't continue hiding and was unable to handle everything that comes along with being a lesbian. She's now married with two children."

"I'm sorry, Nora," I say as I put my arms around her, continuing to look at the fire.

Chucking, she says, "I'm not. She broke my heart, but if she had remained with me, I wouldn't have met you, Vanessa. And what I feel for you is a mature love. You stir me emotionally and sensually. I burn for you; I've never known that before you."

Turning to Nora, I kiss her cheek tenderly and nod, then grin at her as she looks at me. "I understand completely. I loved Jinny very much, but if I had remained with her, I wouldn't have had Anna. She is a pain in my heel a lot of the time, but I love her. And yes, you and I would never have found one another, Nora. And I agree, we have something profound and emotional, baby."

"I haven't been intimate with another woman for three years, Vanessa, so I'm a bit frightened as well. I already know how beautiful it will be. You're everything I've ever imagined wanting in a woman and more than I didn't know I needed," she says, gazing into my eyes.

Threading my fingers through her hair, I look at her lips and then back at her eyes. I see those blue-green gems gazing at my lips. With my hand in her hair, I tenderly pull Nora to me and press my lips against hers. I kiss her briefly and then pull away quickly and say, Nora, I didn't think we'd make love until a few days into our trip, but baby, I don't want to spend another day on this earth without knowing you intimately."

Nora gazes at me and smiles. "Neither do I, darling," she says, pulling me to her and tenderly kissing me. Her lips are soft and full, moving me in ways I remember from years ago. Everything feels completely different with Nora, but the familiarity of loving a woman again washes over me, flooding my senses emotionally and erotically.

Standing, I gaze down at Nora and reach for her hand. She takes it with a smile, standing beside me as she guides us to the bedroom. It's late afternoon, and the sky is already darkening, but the cozy room is illuminated by the flickering firelight of the bedroom fireplace, waiting for us. I pull Nora close and feel her tremble. "Baby, you're trembling," I say lovingly.

"I know, and I hate it," she replies.

Holding her close against me, I whisper, "It's okay, Nora. We'll take it slow, love."

Nora pulls away and gazes at me, unbuttoning my silk blouse. Touching her cheek, I smile and remove the scarf I gave her for Christmas, the one she loves so much, "You've worn this for days," I say with a smile.

Removing my blouse, she asks, "Did I tell you the night I slept with it around me, I slept nude? I didn't want to feel anything on me except you, Vanessa."

Closing my eyes, I feel my heart fall, and I quietly moan and whisper, "Nora." As I open my eyes, I meet her love as I remove her blouse. Pulling her to me, I press my cheek against her ear and whisper, "Did you think of me when you orgasmed, baby?" I ask seductively, wanting her to hear her say yes.

As she unzips my slacks, she leans against my neck and quietly replies, "Yes, I orgasmed all night for you, Vanessa."

"Nora," I gasp, and then I'm suddenly gripped by an erotic intensity that leaves me unable to move. I want nothing more than to be wholly entangled in Nora's embrace—her body, her soul. But as she removes my slacks, I find myself frozen in this charged moment.

Looking up at me, she must sense my hesitation because she steps back and continues undressing, allowing me to sit on the bed and watch her. "Nora, you're absolutely beautiful," I say breathlessly.

"Thank you, darling," she says with a wink. Then she pulls the bedding back on the bed and asks, "Please get in bed with me, Vanessa."

Feeling myself again, I remove my brassiere and crawl in beside Nora. She rises up to gaze at me and then says, "I should have been with older women all along. You're so incredibly gorgeous, Vanessa."

With a laugh, I pull her to me and say, "Hush, I can't stand the thought of you being with other women, especially older ones."

Laughing, she says, "You can't?"

"Not one bit," I say firmly, pulling her warm, nude body against mine. At last, I feel what I've craved all week—*Nora*. I feel her womanness, her youth, and her loving soul. As I grip her body tightly against mine, I run my fingers through her hair as I grab her ass, pulling her against me.

Moaning into her, I feel my erotic desire for her build and surge as I grip her hair. I close my fingers against strands and grasp them tightly. In this erotic passion that's burning for her, I feel the desire to own Nora. I feel possessive of her, "You're mine, Nora," I say with conviction.

"Always, Vanessa," She replies. Then our lips meet in a tender crash, our lips part, and the warmth of her tongue floods my entire body with a passion I've never known. Moving on top of Nora, I brush my tongue gently against hers, wanting to be tender and loving. To memorize every moment of the first time with her. Releasing her lips, I gaze into her captivating eyes and whisper, "I'm in love with you, Nora; I fell for you the moment I met you."

"Vanessa," she says softly as she holds my eyes. You just melted my heart. I want you to be mine forever. I'll never leave or betray you, Vanessa; your heart will always be safe with me," Nora whispers on my lips.

Then, she pulls me against her soft lips and kisses me gently. I love her tenderness and willingness to make love slowly. Nora moves her hands to my face and touches my cheeks, pulls me from her lips, gazes into my soul, and says, "I'm so in love with you, Vanessa. I've wanted to tell you that I love you all week."

Smiling into her heart, I reply, "Having you love me, Nora, is something I almost can't comprehend. But I feel your love."

As she threads her fingers through my hair, she gazes at

me and asks, "Remember the other night when I called you and then had to hang up?

Nodding, I say, "How could I forget that, baby? I wanted to pull you through the phone line and consume you."

Gazing at me, she says, "I had to hang up because *I'm in love with you, Vanessa'* was dangling from my lips, and I was fearful that if I said it, I might lose any chance I had with you.

"Oh, my sweet Nora, you couldn't have lost me, baby—I was already yours. I was so happy when you called. I wept the day you left me. The pain was almost unbearable because I knew I had completely lost my heart to you."

CHAPTER 7

NORA

Smiling into Vanessa's eyes, I ask softly, "Your heart belongs to me?"

"Yes, Nora. For as long as you want me," she replies softly. With a huge grin, I grasp Vanessa's hair and forcefully move on top of her. She laughs and smiles at me "Damn, Nora, you're a bit more dominant in the bedroom than I thought you would be.

"Is that okay?" I ask, grinning at her.

Still laughing, she looks at my lips, then back into my eyes, and replies, "It's more than okay, Nora. It's quite thrilling."

Good, I say with a wink, then gaze at her bosoms. I smile as I cup one in my hand and then move my mouth to her nipple, touch it with the tip of my tongue, then suck it as Vanessa moans. "Yes, baby," she murmurs.

Holding her bosoms in my hands, I pull away, gaze at them, and grin. Vanessa threads her fingers through my hair and then pulls me back to her breasts. As I suck them, she moans and softly says, "Oh yes, Nora." The sound of her voice sends chills through my entire being. My eyes close, and I continue loving her. She keeps her fingers gripped on strands of my hair.

Moving back to her face, I capture her lips in a deep seductive kiss. Vanessa's arms are around my entire body; her strength is intoxicating as she grips me. "Why did you leave your panties on?" I ask in a whisper.

She smiles and replies, "Why do you think, Nora?"

"Oh, I know why," I say as I gaze at her. I just want to hear you tell me why, darling."

With a grin, Vanessa seductively replies, "So you can remove them, my lovely Nora." Gazing at her, I feel my erotic soul burn. Grinning, I reply, "Oh, they're coming off, darling. Don't you worry?"

"Nora," She whispers. "My whole body is in erotic pain and is waiting for you to take me."

As I stay above Vanessa, I hold her eyes as I move my hand down her stomach, then slide slowly down her silk panties. Moving to her sex, I touch it and press softly.

"Oh, Nora, baby." She says breathlessly.

"Yes, Vanessa?" I ask in a whisper, then push my lips against hers. Our tongues meet, and I feel her intense desire as I brush my tongue against hers forcefully. Vanessa meets my intenseness, grips my hair, and pulls me into her.

Pulling away, I immediately move back to her breasts and suck them as I listen to her moan and whisper my name. "Your breasts are gorgeous, Vanessa," I say, then continue sucking them.

"I'm enjoying you sucking them, baby," She says as she gazes at me. Our eyes lock as I suck her nipples and gaze into her eyes. "Yes, Nora. I've wanted you all week."

Without releasing her eyes, I crawl back to her face, my arms extended to keep myself above her. Hovering close, I softly ask, "How many times did you think of me and orgasm last week while I was in your home, Vanessa?"

CHAPTER 7

As Vanessa touches my face, she arches her body upward, needing mine, then replies, "Every night. You should have come to my bed, Nora. I would have given myself willingly. You could have taken me any night you chose."

"Oh god, Vanessa," I say as I close my eyes. Moving to her stomach, I kiss it, then give her long, slow licks as my tongue travels to her nipples. Moving back to her stomach, I kiss my way down her silk panties. My mouth finds her sex. Smelling her, I instinctively say, "My god, your scent is intoxicating."

Vanessa's sexual aroma brings out something primal in me. As I inhale her rich and earthy scent, I pull her panties down slowly, wanting to taste this woman that I crave. After I remove her panties, I clutch them in my hand, move back to her face, look into her eyes, and say, "These are my panties now," I tell her as I put them to my face and smell them.

"Nora, you're an incredible lover. Why do you want my panties? She asks with an erotic grin.

"To show you that you're mine, Vanessa Lord," I say as I place them back to my face, inhaling as I continue gazing into her deep, dark eyes.

With her panties still clutched in my hand, I move back to the scent I just left and find what I desire. Placing my face on her feminine mound, I inhale her again and again. Vanessa parts her legs for me, inviting me into her sacredness. Kissing my way slowly to her clit I feel chills run over me as I listen to her beautiful moans.

My fingers delicately pull at her folds, and I kiss her clit sweetly. Then I move my mouth onto it and reach for her bosoms. Brushing my thumbs across her nipples, I begin moving my tongue slowly back and forth over her clit. "Nora...Nora," Vanessa whispers.

Vanessa sits up, slides her legs to the edge of the bed, and stands. Gazing at me, she gives me a seductive grin. Grinning back, I move to the edge of the bed and whisper, "Come here, darling."

She slowly climbs onto my lap and pushes those wonderful bosoms in my face. "Your breasts are the most glorious ones I've ever seen, Mrs Lord," I say with a grin.

Giggling, Vanessa pulls me to her, "They're all yours, Miss Wolfe." Moaning, I pull her to me and feel her voluptuousness and am overcome with raw desire as I take in her mature body. She whispers in my ear, "Are you going to hold those panties the entire time, love?"

"I told you they're mine now, so I intend to."

"Nora, I was so very wrong about you," she whispers in my ear.

Pulling her ass upward, I move to her opening and gather her warm wetness as she whimpers. Entering her, I gaze into her eyes and ask, "What did you get wrong about me, Vanessa?" Then I push up into her firmly.

Vanessa eases down onto my fingers, deep in her feminine core. With her eyes closed, she softly says, "I thought you were just a kitten." Then she opens her eyes to me and adds, "But you're a damn wildcat."

As I begin thrusting into her slowly, I pull her to me, grip her, still holding her panties, and reply, "Vanessa, a woman like you doesn't want a kitten. What you need is a woman who can be raw and wild with you," I say sternly as I begin thrusting into her.

"Oh god, Nora. Please fuck me," She demands as I keep thrusting into her.

With my left arm wrapped around her back tightly, I pull her to me as I continue with wild, unyielding, forceful thrusts deep into her abyss." Like this, Vanessa," I ask as I keep fucking her.

"Yes, Nora. My god, you're incredible." Making love to

Vanessa got rawer and wilder than I expected for our first time. But It's intoxicating as hell, and so is she.

Changing my rhythm, I slow down and begin giving her deep, slow thrusts. "Oh, Nora, This feels even better, baby."

Placing her panties beside me, I then grab her ass and grip it as I continue fucking her. Vanessa has her arms wrapped tightly around my neck as she rides me, moaning and whimpering my name. "Nora, yes, baby, this feels incredible."

Lying back slowly, I grab her panties, then pull her with me, keeping my fingers deep inside her. Vanessa and I are lying beside one another with my arm underneath her head. Pulling out gently, I move to her clit and press against it with my fingertips, making round soft circles, "Nora," she gasps.

Kissing her deeply, I keep the pressure as I move fluidly against her clit. I feel her beginning to peak. Breaking our kiss, I whisper, "Yes, Vanessa," on her lips.

Threading her fingers through my hair with both hands, she gazes at me as I continue loving her. "I'm close, Nora," she softly says.

"I know, darling."

"Nora, my lovely Nora," she says as she lets go. "I'm coming, baby." I feel her release, as she moans into me. Her clit softens as she comes, and her orgasm fades. I slow down for a moment, then resume pressure again. "Nora, baby, yes," she says as she orgasms once again.

Rising above her, I push my fingers back into her sexual void and begin thrusting as I hover above her. Moving my body and arm in one aggressive fluid movement. With a moan, Vanessa exclaims loudly, "Nora, my god, baby!"

"Do you like how I fuck you, Vanessa?" I ask as my body, arm, and fingers thrust together in a forceful movement deep into her sexual depth. "Open for me, Vanessa," I demand.

"Vanessa moves her legs upward, giving me permission to take her more aggressively. "Yes, darling, let me fuck you," I tell her as I begin to move faster and harder into her. "Do you like this?"

"Yes, Nora. Don't stop, baby. Keep fucking me."

"I can't stop, Vanessa, you're mine," I say sternly.

As I continue, our eyes catch. I whisper, "Come, Vanessa," as I continue loving her forcefully.

She nods, and then her eyes tell me what I need to know. "Yes, darling. Come for me," I say as I gaze at her.

Vanessa nods and then comes again with a loud moan. Her voice rushes through me like a warm wave, then crashes against my feminine soul. As her orgasm ends, she pulls me firmly against her. Easing out slowly, I give her my body to love and be comforted by.

"Nora, my sweet woman, "She softly says. Holding her to me, I pull the covers over us and cuddle into her, wanting to feel her body, her whole essence.

With my head against hers, I whisper, "I love you, Vanessa." She hugs me tightly, sighs, and lightly chuckles. "I couldn't get enough of you, darling. And I could fuck you all over again right now and all night long."

Laughing, Vanessa pulls my face away to gaze at me. "Nora, you're amazing. My god, woman, how did you learn to fuck like that?"

You drive me insane, Vanessa. Isn't it obvious I've wanted you all week?

Nodding and laughing, She grabs my face and replies, "I should have let you fuck me every day in my workspace and every night in my bed, Nora."

"That would have been incredible, Vanessa," I say with a chuckle. Grabbing me forcefully, Vanessa rolls me over and is on top of me instantly.

She gazes at me and smiles tenderly, "I'm so in love with you, Nora. I want to take care of you the rest of my life."

"Vanessa," I whisper. Then I fall silent.

"Will you allow me to do that, Nora?" Her love and words hit me hard. With tears in my eyes, I nod and touch her face tenderly.

"My lovely Nora. I'll give you anything and everything you want, baby."

Grabbing her, I pull her to me and hold her tightly. "Vanessa, all I want is you, darling. If you will promise to always give me that, then yes, I'm yours forever."

CHAPTER 8

VANESSA

"Holding Nora close, I whisper, "Yes, Nora. I'm yours forever, I promise." I gaze into her emerald-blue eyes, threading my fingers through her soft blonde hair. "The depth of what I feel for you is profound, Nora."

Nora whispers, "Tell me, Vanessa."

Holding her body, I rise above her, and our eyes meet. Touching Nora's cheek, I say, "Sweetheart, I feel completely protective of you, as I've said. You are my lover, the woman I love passionately, and my young woman." I run my hands down her youthful body, gazing at her.

"Your young woman? She asks with a giggle. "What exactly does that mean, Vanessa?"

Meeting her eyes, I say, "Nora, that means I'll probably always see you as my young lover, and I love being your older woman. Is that something you can live with?"

"Vanessa, I'd be lying if I said you being older doesn't turn me on, but it isn't why I love you, Darling. But, yes, I think I can live with you seeing me as your young woman," she chuckles.

With a grin, I wink at Nora, whose eyes haven't left mine. "Well, I'm glad we got that straightened out," I say playfully, which makes Nora giggle.

It's actually quite thrilling being your young lover, Vanessa.

Moving my hands slowly down her stomach, I whisper, "What's thrilling about it, Nora?"

Nora moans as I reach her sex and begin massaging the inside of her thighs just beyond her wetness. "Your maturity makes me weak, Vanessa, and I feel completely helpless in your presence at times, like now."

"You feel helpless right now, Nora," I ask seductively.

"I am helpless right now, Vanessa," She says as our eyes lock.

Gazing into Nora's eyes, my fingertips find her wetness. Unwilling to release her lovely eyes, I gather her warm liquid and then move to her clit. As I touch it tenderly, Nora closes her eyes and whispers my name.

Moving my fingers in soft circles Nora opens her eyes again and meets mine. As I increase pressure on her swollen clit she faintly whispers, "Vanessa, I love being your young lover." Her moaning and the words she just spoke send shivers through me.

Looking down at her perfect breasts, I long to feel them in my mouth, so I move down as I continue touching her softly. "Oh, Nora, my lovely woman," I say just before I take one of her nipples in my mouth.

Nora moves her hands to my hair and threads her fingers through strands as she continues whimpering and moaning, "Vanessa….darling."

Under her spell, all I want is to please and love her. Moving back to her wetness, I gaze up at her to read her face. Nora parts her legs for me, and I enter her slowly. She is warm and so ready for me. I close my eyes and whisper,

"Nora," as I push in deeply. My sexual soul surges with a lustful desire to own this young woman.

"Oh, Vanessa, take me, darling,"

As I suck her nipple, I begin pushing deeply into her but feel as though I should be tender with her. Then I hear her repeat, "I said take me, Vanessa."

Rising above her, I gaze into her sweet eyes and see her lustful desire. I nod and then begin giving her intentional, harder thrusts. "Vanessa, yes," she cries out, which sends electric shivers across my body, awakening a rawness in me.

As I gaze at her loveliness, I continue with short but forceful pushes, gaining a rhythm that pleases us both. Nora looks at me and smiles. "Yes, Nora, I'll love you however you need me to, baby," I say as I remain constant with my thrusts.

Remaining above her, I gaze down at her as I continue thrusting into her, "Is this what you need, baby?" I ask in a low, sensual tone.

"Yes, please," she replies as she holds my eyes. Something in me needs to watch her orgasm, so I keep my eyes on her sweet face. As I hover above her, I continue loving her with forceful thrusts. She reaches for my face, holding each side.

"I'm almost there, Vanessa," she quietly whispers.

"Yes, my love," I say as I gaze at her. Nora threads her fingers in my hair, grasps the strands, and then releases.

"Vanessa...I love you," she says as she orgasms. Watching her lose herself to me is emotionally intense and sexually satisfying.

Remaining constant, I keep my thrust and rhythm the same as she continues to fall, "I love you, Nora," I whisper as she closes her eyes. My desire to taste her increases as her orgasm ends. Easing out of her slowly, I move to her warm wetness and hold her thighs as I stop for a moment to smell her. Smelling a woman is something my sexual soul has missed the most. So I inhale Nora, smelling her sweet, clean, and earthy scent. After a moment, I slowly lick and swallow her juices.

"Oh, Vanessa, yes."

Moving my tongue to her clit I glide across it back and forth. Releasing her thighs from my grip, I reach under her leg and then enter her again as before. I know what she wants this time, so I give her all of me. "Oh, Vanessa, yes, baby. Please fuck me."

Hearing those words from my young lover's mouth sends erotic chills and a warm pain throughout my sexual nerve endings. As I glide my tongue over her clit I fuck my lovely Nora with every ounce of strength I have. This young woman is mine, and I'm claiming her. Every forceful push I give Nora gives me the right to own her—love her and take her as my own.

"I'm coming, Vanessa," she moans out to me as I continue loving her. Nora lets out a loud, crying moan. My arm and fingers continue thrusting into her as my tongue continues to love her. As her orgasm ends, I'm determined to continue pleasing her.

Easing out slowly, I move back to her bosoms and suck them greedily as I find her clit with my fingertips again. Pressing against it firmly, I feel an orgasm building again in her, "Come again for me, Nora," I tell her.

Feeling her fingers in my hair again sends shivers over my entire body. My god, how I love this young woman, and I'll never let her go. Moving fluidly and uniformly against her clit sends her to the edge, "Darling, I'm right there. Hold me there, Vanessa, please. Don't allow me to come yet."

"I won't, Nora; I feel you, love, and I won't let you orgasm yet, baby," I say as I feel my sexual center aching with a lustful, intense pain. "Do you like it on the edge, Nora?" I whisper.

"I love you holding me there, Vanessa. Only you could have this power over me, Darling," she says firmly.

Releasing her nipple from my mouth, I move back to her face as I hold her orgasm at bay. Gazing into those eyes, I softly say, "I'll hold you here as long as you wish, Nora."

With a look of vulnerability on her lovely face, she smiles at me and then whispers, "Watch me orgasm, Vanessa."

Nodding, I look at her face and increase the pressure against her clit then I whisper, "I'm watching you, Sweetheart."

Nora's face goes soft as her fingers grip the strands of my hair. This time, she's completely silent, but her face speaks loudly.

"Yes, baby. I feel you coming, Nora." I feel it ending as she closes her eyes, but I want more. I lean in, kiss her sweet lips, and then she opens her eyes.

Looking into her eyes, I softly say, "Will you come again for your older woman, baby?" Nora's body responds to my words instantly. She immediately begins to orgasm again as I smile at her and watch her fall once again for me.

"Oh, Vanessa," she cries out. "I'll always come for you." After she climaxes, I move close to her and kiss her cheek.

Pulling her into my arms, I whisper, "Nora, I love you."

She places her arms around my neck, holds me tightly, and sighs. "I'm so in love with you, Vanessa. Never let go of me. I need you, Darling."

Holding her tightly, I reply, "Nora, you belong to me. How could I ever let you go?"

Nora sighs, then replies, "I love belonging to you, Vanessa, and being your young lover."

"Come here and let me hold you close," I say lovingly. Nora moves into my arms. "Yes, baby, you feel amazing."

"Vanessa?"

"Yes, Nora?"

"No one has ever made love to me the way you just loved me," she says softly.

Holding her face with my hand, I kiss her head and reply, "I'll always make love to you from my heart and my erotic desires for you, Nora."

"Vanessa, how did you know what I needed?" She asks.

"Your body spoke to me, Nora; I just listened." I pause for a moment before adding, "The way you made love to me was unlike anything I've ever known, baby. We must both be good at listening—or perhaps we're just completely in love," I chuckle.

Nora laughs softly in response. "I think it's both." She props herself up, looking deeply into my eyes. "Vanessa, having a woman like you so in love with me is incredible," she says sweetly.

Smiling, I brush my fingertips against her lips and wink at her before pulling her back into a tight embrace. As I hold Nora in my arms, I continue to shut out the world as I've done over the past few years, knowing I'll never give her up.

Years ago, I lost the only other woman I've ever loved because of society; I'll be damned if I'll lose Nora. She wants me and is committed, and she has a strong will, unlike Jinny. For that reason alone, I believe in Nora and in our love.

As I awake to the morning light, thoughts of making love to Nora travel back to me, and I smile. Despite being in my arms all night, I find her missing from our bed.

Slipping on my robe, I walk into the living room and see her in the kitchen. Her back is to me as she pours coffee. Gazing at her lovely blonde hair, I grin and approach her, encircling her from behind. I feel her giggle, so I grasp her tightly and ask, "What are you giggling about, Nora Wolfe?"

"You! You make me so happy, Vanessa." She quickly turns around and grabs me with her arms around my neck. Gripping her waist, I pull her tightly. "Never let me go, Vanessa. I can't lose you."

Threading my fingers through her hair, I say, "Nora, what's wrong, baby?"

"I just need to hear you say it again," she replies firmly.

"Nora," I whisper against her. "Baby, I told you that you belong to me, and I'll never let you go, and I meant that." I feel her nodding.

Pulling away to gaze at her face, I see a bit of uncertainty. Taking her hand, I walk us to the couch, and we sit. Interlacing my fingers with hers, I say, "Nora, I want you to know something." She nods, and her eyes are fixed on me.

CHAPTER 9

NORA

Gazing at Vanessa, I see the love in her eyes for me —the same loving eyes that have loved me the last week and especially the last few days.

Smiling at me, she says, "Nora, a few years ago I sold a business I had owned for several years. It was a textile business, and we had started making uniforms and other military apparel. The orders and government contracts I procured during the war gave my business a considerable revenue boost and a favorable company evaluation.

Knowing that the war wouldn't last forever, I decided to sell it at its peak, and I did. It netted me a substantial amount of money. This was after Thomas and I had divorced, so the money I received was entirely mine and still is.

"That's incredible, Vanessa. And I'm glad you didn't have to share it with Anna's dad," I laugh. Then add, "I think I know what you're getting at, Vanessa. I think you're trying to tell me you don't have to answer to anyone."

Kissing my cheek, she laughs and says, "Yes, Nora, but it's more than that. It also means that you and I, as a couple, don't have to answer to anyone, baby."

"Well, Vanessa. I still want to keep my photography career," I reply.

"Of course you do, baby. I wouldn't have it any other way. But, let's get back to your initial fear when I walked into the kitchen," she says softly.

Gazing into her eyes, I ask, "What about Anna, Vanessa?"

Nodding, I see that she understands my fear. "Nora, Anna has chosen to live her life without me. Thank goodness she brought you home to spend Christmas with me, but her real reason was to reunite with her friends for the holidays. Wouldn't you agree?" She asks.

"Yes, and I almost hated her for that once I met you. You're so lovely, Vanessa, I hate that she takes a Mother like you for granted. I lost mine years ago, so I can't understand why she doesn't appreciate you."

Pulling me close, Vanessa whispers, "I'm sorry you lost your parents, Nora. When you spoke about them at Christmas and the drive up, I could tell you loved them so much."

"I miss them dreadfully at times, Vanessa."

"Nora, I'll always take care of you, but I want you to have the freedom to live your life how you choose."

Snuggling into her neck, I kiss it and ask, "So there isn't one reason why you would ever let me go?

"No, Nora. Baby, you're mine, and I'll always love and protect you for as long as I live."

With a reassuring sigh, I relax and surrender to Vanessa's loving words, knowing that this older woman indeed loves me and has no intentions of ever letting me go.

After a moment, she says, "Nora, I will tell Anna about us, and I don't expect it to go well. But nothing that girl could ever say to me would ever push me into releasing you. She doesn't have the right to tell me who I choose to love. Don't you ever forget that? Okay?"

Pulling away from her, I nod. "I felt like it may come down to you having to choose between us," I say softly.

Touching my face, Vanessa looks deeply into my eyes and replies, "Nora, if it ever came to that, then I'd choose you every single time, baby."

"You would?" I ask, almost shocked.

"Of course, Nora. Baby, you're my love—my lover. The woman I want to spend the rest of my life with, and no one in this world could ever make me choose anyone but you."

Smiling, I get onto my knees and fall into Vanessa's arms, hugging her with laughter. "So you're my older woman forever, Mrs. Lord?" I ask as I giggle.

"Forever, Nora," she replies sweetly.

Vanessa pulls me tightly, grabs my ass, and pulls me to her lips for an intense morning kiss. Breaking our kiss, I say, "I love you rubbing my ass, Mrs Lord."

"You do?" she asks seductively. "I love your ass, Miss Wolfe. I think it will be my breakfast. Lay across me, and let me make sure that's what I want."

Giggling, I lay across her lap as she asked. Rubbing my ass, she then goes beneath my robe and says, "Hmmm, you're still nude, you naughty girl."

As I relax on her lap, I feel her soft hands massaging my ass, "That feels unreal, Vanessa. My god, your power over me is unreal," I say breathlessly.

Glancing back at her, I say, "Take me back to bed, Vanessa. Food can wait; the things I want you to do to me can't."

Gripping my hair and my ass Vanessa says, "I'll do anything you ask of me, Nora. Any desire you ever have, I will always quench, baby." She says with a wink.

"Damn," I whisper. "Are all older women like this?" I ask.

Vanessa laughs and says, "I doubt it, baby. But this one's different when it comes to you, and that's all you need to know." Then, with a playful swat on my ass, she adds, "Come on, my young lover."

Jumping up, I run to the bed and dive into it, waiting eagerly. Vanessa stops at the doorway, smiles, and crosses her arms, leaning casually against the doorframe. Lying on my tummy, I gaze at her with a playful grin. "Are you coming, ma'am?" I tease.

"Oh, yes," she replies, her voice full of warmth. "I just wanted to take a moment to admire you, lying there waiting for me, Nora." Our eyes meet, and in that look, I know without a doubt that this woman will never let me go, just as she's promised.

As I lean against the kitchen cabinet, fidgeting with my Rolleiflex—the camera that cost me a small fortune but serves as my vehicle for making money, I watch Vanessa paint. Walking to her, I stand beside her and touch her back. "That's beautiful, darling," I say warmly.

"Thank you, love," she says, giving me a sweet glance.

"Is this for me?" I ask with a giggle.

"Yes, I'm painting these snow-capped mountains just for you, Nora. You wanted snow, baby, so I'm giving you snow."

Shaking my head, I continue touching her back, and then I lean in to smell her. "I love your smell, Vanessa. You gave me a welcome hug when I first entered your home, and your scent lingered on me all day and that night, darling."

Vanessa looks at me and smiles. I grin at her and whisper, "Yes." against her ear.

She laughs, resumes painting, and asks, "Yes, what?"

"Yes, I fantasized about you that night and orgasmed as I smelled your scent on me, Vanessa Lord."

Vanessa laughs softly and asks, "What was your fantasy,

Nora?" she asks playfully as she paints the snow on the mountaintops.

Well, do you remember showing me your workspace that first day?" I ask softly. Vanessa grins at me and nods as she continues painting.

"Let's just say it involved me in a very compromising position on that sofa in your workspace," I say as I kiss her head.

"Nora, I am making great progress here, so you better go outside with that camera right now. Otherwise, you're going to end up in that compromising position you fantasized about on that sofa over there in front of this warm fire," she says with a grin.

"So, in other words, if I don't leave you alone, you're going to make the first fantasy I ever had about you come true." With a nod, she looks at me. Our eyes catch, and in a flash, I fall instantly in love with her all over again.

Walking to the door, I turn the knob and glance over my shoulder at her. Our eyes meet, and with all the sincerity in my heart, I say, "I love you, Vanessa Lord." Then, turning away, I step outside to greet the briskness of the day.

As I wander through the stillness, I marvel at the beauty of these mountains. How starkly different they look this time of year—the trees left barren for the winter, stripped of their leaves, a sharp contrast to the lush green of summer and the vibrant colors of fall.

Choosing black-and-white film, I load my Rolleiflex, knowing it's the only film stock capable of capturing the bleakness and raw loneliness of the Blue Ridge Mountains in winter—a place I've cherished for as long as I can remember.

The memories flood back—countless trips here with my parents before their tragic death in a car crash several years ago. My heart aches, and the sorrow seeps into my soul. Tears well up, and suddenly, these mountains feel haunted, a reminder of all I've lost. The pain strikes swiftly, over-whelming me.

Walking to a tree, I let it catch me and begin weeping. It's been at least a year since I've had one of these crushing moments of grief, but they still have the power to consume me without warning. Lost in tears, I feel Vanessa's loving arms wrap around me from behind.

"Nora, my love," she whispers softly.

"Come back inside," she gently urges, pulling me closer, her warmth surrounding me. Once inside, the fire's heat and Vanessa's embrace envelop me, easing the sorrow as I lean into her love.

She pulls me to the couch, taking me in her arms lovingly, holding me against her breasts. She remains silent, letting me grieve my immense loss. After a few minutes, the tears subside, and I wipe my face with a handkerchief, softly saying, "I'm better now." But Vanessa doesn't let go.

As she holds me, a realization dawns on me. I sit up, look into her eyes, and say, "You're my family now, Vanessa." She nods, smiling as her fingers glide through my hair.

"Yes, Nora. I am definitely your family now, baby." Nodding, I laugh; the warmth of her love makes me feel like I'm no longer alone. Vanessa is my home. As I gaze into the fire, a smile spreads across my face, and my soul feels lighter.

Looking back at her, I say, "I think that was my last cry, my final purge from losing them. It always hits me out of nowhere, but this time, you caught me, darling."

Vanessa tucks a few strands of hair behind my ear and asks gently, "Are you okay now, baby?" I smile, nodding at her, then lean in to kiss her softly.

"Yes, I'm fine. Thank you for catching me." Sitting back, I ask, "How did you know, Vanessa?"

Smiling, she replies, "I've been watching you, Nora, ever

since you left. I confess I've got it quite bad for you, my young love."

Laughing, I kiss her cheek, then pull back and gaze at her. "It all makes sense now, Vanessa."

With a curious look, Vanessa asks sincerely, "What makes sense, baby?"

"You," I say, glancing back at the fire. "They sent me to you, Vanessa. I've always believed there are no coincidences. They knew I would fall in love with you and that you would love me forever."

Wrapping her arms around me, she softly asks, "Do you believe that, Nora?"

"Of course," I say, resting against her. "I believe it with all of my heart."

CHAPTER 10

VANESSA

O ver the past few days, I've lived and breathed Nora just as I've wanted. As we walk the trail up to *Blowing Rock*, she slips her arm around mine and gives me that sweet smile that melts me every time. "I'm glad you brought a couple of canvases to sketch the scenery. I have seven shots left on this roll of film, and I intend to use six of them on you, darling," she says, smiling.

Grinning, I respond, "Nora, don't you think the scenery at the top deserves more than just one shot, love?"

"Of course, darling," she says, winking at me. "When we reach the top, you'll be there, so the view will most certainly be worthy of all seven shots."

I chuckle, glancing around to see if anyone else is nearby before pulling her close to kiss her cheek. "You're too much, sweetheart," I say, my heart swelling with happiness.

As we reach the summit of *Blowing Rock*, Nora grabs my hand and shouts, "Vanessa! Look at this!" Her excitement radiates through me, thrilling me even more than the raw beauty of the sweeping landscape below. "Oh, how breath-taking!" she exclaims.

"It's magnificent, Nora," I say, gazing in awe at the spectacular view. As I glance at her, I see her peering through the viewfinder of her camera, a smile illuminating her face. Walking up behind her, I place my hand gently on her waist, a concern for her safety tugging at my heart. "Baby, please step back a bit; if you slipped, my whole world would crumble."

Nora glances over her shoulder at me, our eyes locking in a moment that feels powerfully intimate. With both hands resting on her waist, she steps back toward me. Leaning her head against mine, she softly says, "Being this important to a woman like you, Vanessa, is something I'm going to need time to get used to."

Remaining in this intense, loving moment, I put my arms around her waist, rest my head against hers, and close my eyes. I feel her energy, the briskness of the late afternoon, and my immense love for her.

Releasing Nora, I gaze out over the expansive vista, pick up a canvas, and begin sketching the landscape blanketed in a pristine layer of white snow. Below, the valleys are shrouded in a soft, ethereal fog, giving the impression that the mountains are floating on a bed of clouds. I take mental notes of the cool colors that embody the essence of winter.

As I sketch, the sun begins to set above the cool blue mountains, transforming the sky into a canvas of soft pastels —pinks, purples, and blues blending seamlessly together. These delicate hues hang above the cold mountain peaks, casting a warm, haunting glow over the icy and tranquil landscape of the *Blue Ridge Mountains.*

Excitedly, I grab my other canvas, turn to my right, and start sketching rapidly as the light begins to fade. My heart swells with love for Nora and the breathtaking landscape that I can't wait to bring to life on canvas. I gaze once more mentally, absorbing the cool blues and soft whites of the snow against the warm hues of the setting sun, etching them into my memory for when I finally lay paint to canvas.

As I sketch, I feel Nora close. Stopping for a moment to glance at her, I see her camera in hand, pointing directly at me. I give her a warm smile and hear the shutter click just as I catch her peeking above the camera at me. Our eyes meet, and I can't help but be captivated by her immense beauty, framed against the incredible backdrop of these ancient mountains.

Nora walks to me with a sweet smile that lights up my heart. "May I look at your sketches? She asks sweetly.

"Yes, you may, love," I reply as I continue working on the second sketch.

"Oh, Vanessa, these are going to be beautiful when you paint them," she says, her lovely face filled with excitement.

"When I finish painting them, I'm going to hang them in our bedroom, Nora," I say softly, then glance at her. Watching her expression shift from excitement to an intense, serious gaze moves me sensually and emotionally.

Nora gives me a slight nod before looking out over the vast expanse, clearly needing a moment to ponder my statement. After a pause, she turns her head toward me and, almost whispering, says, "*Our* bedroom, Vanessa?"

Continuing my sketching, I ask, "Do you like the sound of that, Nora?" With her back still turned, I see her nodding, which makes me smile. "Come here, baby," I urge her.

Nora walks slowly to me, our eyes merging as I see the look in hers. She stops just before reaching me, raises her camera, and clicks off another shot. "I needed to capture you at this moment, Vanessa." Then she moves closer, gazes deeply into my eyes, and says, "Yes, Vanessa, these will be beautiful in our bedroom."

As my heart swells, a broad smile fills my face, and I suddenly feel twenty years younger with Nora next to me.

She is standing close, gazing out at the grand bleakness of this magical view. "Are you cold, sweetheart," I ask.

With her somber gaze still lost in the mountain view, I glance around again to ensure no one is close. Gently sitting my canvas down, I pull her to me and ask, "Why did that seem to make you sad, Nora?"

Turning her beautiful face to mine, she says, "I'll never forget this moment, Vanessa." Leaning closer, she adds, "I'm not sad, darling. I'm just overwhelmed by how that sounded —*our bedroom*."

After a moment, Nora picks up one of my canvases and says, "We better head back, darling. It's getting dark, and I don't want you out in this damp cold much longer, especially with that cough you've had since this morning."

"I'm fine, Nora," I assure her, slipping my arm around her waist. I pull her close as we walk the trail back to the car. A comfortable silence settles between us, broken only by the crunch of snow beneath our shoes and the chill of the winter air around us.

When I get in the car, I crank it, turn the heat on, turn to Nora, and ask, "Did you get cold, baby?"

Smiling at me, she says, "No, I have on this gorgeous peacoat you bought me days ago, so I'm toasty." Grinning at her, I put the car in reverse, glancing at her intermittently. I still can't believe Nora is mine and that she loves me. As I shift the car into drive, I reach for her hand, our fingers intertwining. I chuckle to myself, knowing what I have.

After a moment, Nora slides over next to me, lays her head on my shoulder, and snuggles against me. My heart feels like it could explode as I put my arm around her and pull her tight. "This blue peacoat looks beautiful on you, Nora, especially with your flaxen blonde hair."

"I love it, Vanessa, especially because you bought it for

me. I feel as though I'm wrapped in your nurturing love. You're so very good to me, darling."

Cautiously watching the curvy mountain roads, I take a moment to kiss Nora's soft hair and smell it. "You're kind to me, Nora; you have a heart as golden as your lovely hair, baby."

When I enter the cabin, despite the warm, inviting fire, a chill sweeps over me. As I walk toward the couch, a sudden coughing fit seizes me, and I can't seem to stop.

"Vanessa, darling, that cough is getting worse," Nora says, her voice tight with worry. "It might have been foolish of me to take you out into the damp air, especially on that walk up to *Blowing Rock*."

"Nora, I'll be fine. It's just a cold, I'm sure. Please don't worry about me."

"Well, I am concerned, Vanessa, and I'm glad you enjoy your tea. I will make you a hot cup with honey. Come to the sofa and lie down while I make the tea."

Lying down, I glance at the fire as I continue to cough. I don't feel well, my energy felt almost depleted as I entered the cabin. Sitting up, I say, "Nora, I'm going to bed, I think it would be best if I rested there."

Walking back to me with that same concerned look, she says, "Of course, come on, I'll put you to bed and bring your tea when it's ready."

After Nora tucks me in, I keep my eyes on her. I feel unwell, but watching this gorgeous young woman seems to make it better. Nora places another log on the fire, walks over, kisses my lips, and then says, "I'll be right back with your tea, darling."

CHAPTER 11

NORA

T he following morning, as I wake, I immediately reach for Vanessa. She coughed most of the night and was very restless. Despite several cups of tea, her cough remains persistent, and if anything, it is getting worse.

She opens her eyes as I touch her face and says sweetly, "Good morning, my lovely angel."

"Vanessa! You're burning up with fever!" I say in a frantic tone. Running to the bathroom, I quickly grab a washcloth, immerse it in cool water, and then take it back to Vanessa. As I place it on her forehead, I sit beside her. "Darling, you have me worried. I've gotta find a doctor. You coughed all night, and now you have a fever."

"Nora, it's most likely just a cold or perhaps the flu, love. Don't make a fuss."

"Oh, I'm going to make a fuss, just like you would if I were lying here ill," I say sternly, then walk to the living room to find the phone book.

I just called a nearby doctor and told him about her symptoms and how we had traveled to *Blowing Rock* yesterday. He said he would drop by within a couple of hours. He seemed concerned, which left me feeling quite uneasy.

Sitting at Vanessa's bedside, I hold her hand between mine. She doesn't open her eyes but gives me a tender smile. I can't help but notice her breathing sounds a bit labored.

Vanessa opens her brown eyes and softly says, "Nora, I'm a bit cold love." I immediately grab the blankets from the other bedroom and cover her. Then I replace the washcloth with another cool one as I watch her.

"Darling, I'm going to make you another cup of hot tea with lemon," I say as I kiss her lips tenderly.

With her eyes still closed, she whispers, "Nora, you have the sweetest lips. I wanted to kiss them from the moment I first met you." Then she smiles and drifts off.

Tears fill my eyes seeing the woman I love so ill. I feel helpless, knowing all I can offer is more hot tea. Hopefully, the doctor won't be too long because I don't like how she looks.

As I prepare Vanessa's tea, I hear her coughing again. Taking the tea to the bedroom, I see her sitting up and coughing. "Here, darling, drink this," I say in a concerned voice.

Vanessa takes the tea and drinks it, then immediately begins coughing again. Her cough seems different; it has a rattle about it. Taking the teacup, I place it on the nightstand and take her in my arms. "I can't stand this, Vanessa. You have me so worried. I wish that doctor would get here."

"I'll be okay, love. I just need some rest," she says as she lies back down. As I gaze at her, I hear a vehicle pull up to the cabin. I rush to the door and see a middle-aged man exiting a car. He's short, a bit plump, and has gray hair that immediately reminds me of Einstein.

As he enters the cabin, I say, "Thank you for coming, Doctor Guest. She's in the bedroom."

Touching Vanessa, her brown eyes open, and she gives me a tender smile. Then I wink at her and say, "Doctor Guest, this is my Mother, Vanessa. Mother, this is Doctor Guest; he's here to check on you."

With a knowing expression in her eyes, she says, "Thank you, Nora."

After a series of questions about her breathing, taking vital signs, and listening to her breathing through his stethoscope, he determined that she had Pneumonia.

Sitting on the other side of the bed, I ask, "How did she get pneumonia, doctor?"

As he rummages through his black bag, he hesitates for a moment and then says, "Most likely, the damp air yesterday contributed along with possible pathogens, which can infect the lungs."

"Pathogens? What are pathogens, doctor?" I ask concerned.

After hesitating, he pulls out a book of blank prescription pads and replies, "Pneumonia is caused by tiny germs, called pathogens, that infect the lungs. However, it can be treated effectively with the right medication." Then, he begins scribbling on one of the pages of his pad.

"What type of medications?" I ask.

"Penicillin, " he says firmly as he tears off the prescription from his pad, hands it to me, and then returns it to his black bag.

The doctor tells Vanessa to rest and that he will check on her in a couple of days. Then he walks me into the living room and says, "Make sure your Mother gets plenty of fluids like herbal teas and clear broth. Also, she needs to eat to keep up her strength."

"We have plenty of tea here but only a few other essentials. We are here vacationing, so we usually eat out."

He nods and says, "There is a pharmacy in town. You

might want to get some cough medication to ease her symptoms and acetaminophen to keep her fever down. I've just given her some, so it will most likely bring the fever down temporarily."

"Okay, I will go into town right away and get the medication. How often should I give her the acetaminophen?"

As he brushes his fingers through his disheveled hair, he gazes at me and quickly says, "It comes in 325 mg, so give her 1 to 2 tablets every 4 to 6 hours." Then he steps sideways a bit, rests his chin on his fist, and asks, "There isn't a humidifier here, is there?"

Scanning the cabin, I glance at him with a soft chuckle and reply, "I doubt it. Can I get one at the pharmacy?" I ask as I search his eyes for worry.

"Yes, they have them there. It would be very beneficial because it produces moist air that will make her breathing easier and more comfortable, " he says as he walks slowly to the front door.

"I'll immediately get this prescription filled along with some food and the other items you mentioned. Will she be okay here alone while I'm gone?"

He pats my shoulder softly and says, "Yes, it shouldn't take you more than an hour or so; she'll be okay."

"Thank you, Doctor Guest, I appreciate you coming out here so quickly," I say sincerely.

"You're welcome, dear. Just keep an eye on her. I'll check back in a few days. If her condition worsens, please call me. We might need to reassess her." Nodding my head, I open the front door and bid him goodbye.

Walking back to Vanessa, I stand and gaze at her. Her uncomfortable expression makes my heart ache. Sitting on her bedside, I touch her cheek, then lean down and kiss her lips again.

Her brown eyes open for me, and she smiles, still wanting

to show me she's okay, but I know she isn't. "Darling, I have to go into town to get your medication, food, and other supplies. I shouldn't be more than an hour or so," I say tenderly.

"Okay, baby. Don't be too long because I'll miss you," She says in a sleepy, loving tone that breaks my heart.

"Leaning to her face, I kiss her cheek and say, "Just rest, darling. I'll be back as quickly as I can." Then I grab my peacoat and her car keys and dash out of the cabin.

Driving into town, I find myself anxious and scared. I know Vanessa will most likely be okay, but I've heard of many people passing away from Pneumonia. Shaking my head, I remind myself, *That won't happen to my beautiful woman because I'm not losing her.* I've waited forever for a woman like Vanessa, and I'll be damned if I let anything happen to her.

~

Vanessa

"Nora...Nora?" I quietly call out, but all I hear is silence. As I begin coughing, I suddenly remember Nora mentioning she had to go into town. Lying here, I feel somewhat disoriented, my mind foggy. Pulling the extra covers up close that Nora brought from the other bedroom, I snuggle down and try to get warm.

I hear the crackle and popping of the fireplace, knowing that my lovely Nora is keeping the room warm and comfortable for me despite my chill. A dull ache courses through my muscles, leaving me completely fatigued. I can't remember ever being so ill.

All I wanted on this trip was to spend every moment loving Nora, but now here I am, sick with Pneumonia. If there is anything that will alert Nora to our age difference, having Pneumonia might do it. My mind races, and I think *I don't want her to see me sick like this. This isn't the Vanessa she knows.*

Another coughing fit attacks me as I hear the car pull up. Sitting up, I hear the front door open, and Nora immediately walks into the bedroom. "Vanessa, darling, you should lie down," she says, her voice tinged with concern.

"I have been, baby," I say as she rushes to me. Nora grabs me tightly and holds me with a nurturing strength that surprises me but is quite comforting. "I love you holding me, Nora."

Nora threads her fingers through my hair and gently holds a few strands. "I'm going to take care of you, Vanessa. You're my older woman, remember?"

With a chuckle, I say, "Yes, I do, Nora, and nothing proves that like a good case of pneumonia." We both laugh as Nora keeps a tight grip on me.

I'm somewhat overwhelmed by this young woman's nurturing strength, but I shouldn't be. Nora has shown me in the bedroom that she is indeed a woman and has rendered me almost helpless at times with her aggressiveness.

"Vanessa, I'm going to take care of you, and you're going to be fine, darling," she says as she releases me and then looks into my eyes.

With a smile, I touch her lips as I gaze into her blue-green eyes and whisper, "I love your Emerald Coast eyes, Nora Wolfe. They've captivated me since I met you."

Nora gives me a grin and asks, "Will you take me there in the spring?"

Keeping my fingers on her lips, I softly reply, "Yes, Nora. It's not that far from our home in Savannah, about 300 miles or so. I'll paint you a beach scene. Would you like that?"

Nora's eyes immediately pool with tears. "Why do your lovely eyes suddenly have tears, Nora?"

"You know why, Vanessa," she replies.

"Perhaps I do, but love. The only way we can have that bedroom together is if you come and live with me, Nora," I say as I feel myself slipping into slumber. "I meant every word of that, Nora," I whisper as I drift off quietly.

CHAPTER 12

NORA

As I watch Vanessa drift off, I quickly dry my eyes, then lean in and kiss her cheek as I smell her intoxicating aroma. It's so alluring, especially during lovemaking. A hint of her perfume still lingers on her skin, mingled with her unique body scent.

After setting the humidifier to a gentle mist, I toss another log on the fire, watching the flames dance and flicker. I bring a rocking chair from the living room beside the bed, making myself comfortable as I sip hot tea.

Glancing at Vanessa, sleeping peacefully, my heart swells with concern and affection. I made sure she took all the medication the doctor prescribed, along with a warm bowl of chicken broth. The cough medicine has eased her discomfort, and unlike last night, she appears to be resting soundly.

Setting my teacup on the nightstand, I rock slowly, keeping my eyes on her. I'd love to crawl next to her, but it's better to stay upright and attentive. Listening to the soft humming of the humidifier and the crackling of the fire, I find myself enchanted in this moment as I care for her. In the softness of the moment, I find myself drifting off gently.

Startled awake by Vanessa's worsening cough, I rush quickly to her side. As I pour another spoonful of cough syrup, I hold her warm face and whisper, "Open your mouth, darling." Laying the cough medicine and spoon back on the nightstand, I take Vanessa in my arms again and hold her close to me. "How do you feel?" I ask soothingly.

"Not good, love," she faintly replies.

"Darling, I am caring for you, but a hospital is eight miles away. If you don't get better, then that's where I'm taking you."

"Okay, Nora, but I prefer you care for me here in our warm cabin."

With a light chuckle, I reply, "That's what I want too, darling. But if you get much worse, I'll be forced to take you there." As I pull away, I look into her eyes. She looks so weak and unwell, and my heart twists in knots.

As she lies back, I sit beside her for a moment, our eyes meeting. "Just rest, and let me take care of you, darling", I say. She smiles and then gives me one of her sweet winks, which melts my heart.

Rocking softly next to Vanessa, I am in contemplative prayer, fully aware of my Creator's presence. Speaking with God, I know it may get darker before her body is healed, but I am quieted by the peace that only faith can bring.

Despite the medication, tea, and broth, Vanessa seems to become worse as the night lingers. Pacing the living room, I glance at the phone, knowing I should call Anna to let her know that I've decided to take her to the hospital.

How am I even going to explain why her mother and I are in *Blowing Rock* together. I don't want to call her, and Vanessa may not like this either, but I feel she needs to know her mother is very ill.

After the operator dials her number, I hear it ringing. I'm nervous as hell because I have no idea how Anna is going to respond.

"Hello," She says in a groggy tone.

"Anna, it's Nora," I say in a low tone.

"Anna? My gosh, it's one a.m. Are you okay?" she asks in a concerned voice.

Taking a deep breath, I say it all in one long sentence, "Anna, your mother and I took a trip to *Blowing Rock,* North Carolina, several days ago. She now has pneumonia and is very ill. I'm going to take her to the hospital as soon as I hang up, but I wanted you to know." Then I inhale and close my eyes, fearful of her response.

"Why are the two of you together, Nora?" She pauses, then adds, "Oh god... don't answer that. I think I already know," her tone laced with exasperation.

"What hospital are you taking her to?" she asks angrily.

"It's Watauga County Hospital in Boone, North Carolina," I say, and then the phone goes silent.

"How sick is she, Nora?" She asks anxiously.

"She's gotten much worse over the past few hours, so I wanted you to know," I respond as the phone goes silent.

"I'm getting up now and driving there. Tell Mother that I'm coming, " she says in a hurried voice. Then she adds, "Please take care of her, Nora."

"I am Anna. You may not want to hear this, but I love her more than anything on this earth," then I begin to cry. Anna is silent but remains on the line.

After a moment, she growls, "Well, I guess this explains why the two of you spent so much time together during Christmas. Dammit, Nora." Then she hangs up.

Placing the receiver back in the cradle, I cover my face

with my hands and nod slowly. I don't want her here, but I know it was right to call her.

Walking back into the bedroom, I sit on the edge of the bed and gently touch Vanessa's face. She immediately whispers, "Nora, my love." My heart breaks seeing her so ill.

"Darling, I'm going to take you to the hospital. As I mentioned earlier, it isn't that far away."

Opening her eyes, she says, "I just want to stay here with you, Nora."

"Vanessa, I know you do, but your fever seems constant, and I'm scared, darling."

She touches my face softly and replies, "Okay, Nora, baby. I don't want you to be scared. Just bring me my coat, and we'll go."

"I have it right here; I'll help you stand up."

After getting Vanessa in the car, I get in the driver's seat and say, "Lay in my lap, darling." With my fingers threaded through her hair, I take off toward the hospital, knowing this is the best option.

Upon admitting Vanessa, the doctor quickly assessed her condition, placed her in a room, and started her on IV fluids for hydration while administering injections of penicillin. They're allowing me to stay with her since I told them she is my mother.

The nurse has been in and out of Vanessa's room several times to monitor her vital signs. After she leaves, I lean down and kiss Vanessa on her forehead. I hear her faintly whisper, "My lovely Nora," which breaks my heart.

As I gaze at her, my heart twists, and I feel on the verge of breaking down, but I remain strong for her. Leaning again, I whisper, "I love you, Vanessa Lord." She smiles sweetly before drifting off.

Sitting in a chair beside her, I hold her hand and kiss it gently. Pulling her hand to my face, I tenderly rub my cheek against it, then lay my head on the edge of the mattress, continuing to hold her hand.

Looking up, I see the doctor coming into the room, and I stand to introduce myself to him. "I'm Doctor Yancey," he says, then pauses, puts his stethoscope earpieces in, and begins listening to her chest.

After a moment, he says, "I'm glad you brought your mother in. I see in my notes that Doctor Guest came out initially and treated her."

"Yes, he came out yesterday and gave her penicillin, and I've been giving her broth, hot tea, and acetaminophen," I reply.

"That's exactly what she needed. We are going to continue to monitor her vitals, and she might need oxygen therapy. We must keep her hydrated and comfortable. Please know we will do everything we can to manage her symptoms and help her to get better.

After he leaves, I lay my head against Vanessa's bed, wanting her to know I'm beside her. Closing my eyes, a million thoughts flood my mind. I revisit our walk up to *Blowing Rock* and think of what she said to me as she sketched the scenic view:*When I finish painting them, I'm going to hang them in our bedroom, Nora,*

Waking to the sun streaming through the small window, I stand and then sit on the edge of Vanessa's bed and gaze at her. Touching her face, I notice she is still warm but not as bad as she was when I brought her in. Kissing her hand, she opens her eyes, smiles at me, and says, "I love you, Nora."

With tearful eyes, I whisper, "I love you, Vanessa. You and I are going to have a beautiful life together, so you have to get well for me."

Vanessa touches my face softly and replies, "You're so loving, Nora. I'll get better, love. Remember, I promised to take you to the Emerald Coast in the spring. Nodding with tears in my eyes, I can't help but smile.

Looking into her eyes, I say, "Vanessa, you got very ill late last night, so before I brought you to the hospital, I called Anna.

She furrows her brow then nods, "It's okay, Nora. I'd prefer she wasn't coming, but I understand why you called her, baby. Well, we'll deal with it when she arrives." she says with a chuckle.

"Darling, she wanted me to tell you she's coming," I say softly. Vanessa nods, then closes her eyes and drifts off lightly.

CHAPTER 13

VANESSA

Opening my eyes, I turn my head and see Nora's head lying against the mattress of my bed. Reaching for her, I thread my fingers through her soft, flaxen blonde hair and smile. Nora raises her head to me and softly asks, "How are you, darling?"

With depleted strength, I simply smile at her, wanting her to feel my love. Hearing the door open, I look and see Anna entering. She walks to my bedside, looks at Nora's fingers intertwined with mine, and then gives Nora an angry glare.

"Anna?" I say softly.

"Yes, I'm here, Mother. How do you feel?" she asks in a displeased tone.

"Not good, Anna, but I'll be okay. You didn't have to come, but I'm glad you're here," I reply, reaching my hand for hers. She takes it and then gives me a kiss on the cheek.

Nora stands and says, "Vanessa, I'm going to the waiting area. I'll be close if you need me," keeping her eyes on me.

With Anna beside us, I smile at Nora and say, "Okay, baby, don't be long."

After Nora leaves, Anna stares at me for what seems like forever, then says, "Mother, I don't understand."

Clasping her hand between both of mine, I softly say, "I don't expect you to. You haven't understood me for years, but I love you, Anna."

Shaking her head, she replies, "What does that mean?"

Gazing at her, I reply, "Anna, despite you and I being close when you were young, somehow along the way, our paths divided, and the distance between us has only grown wider," I say as I begin to cough.

As I cough, Anna grabs some tissue, sits beside me on the bed, and says, "I know this isn't the right time to discuss this; I just want you to get better." She gazes out the window and says, "I do love you, Mother."

After my coughing subsides, I reply, "I know you love me, Anna." She looks back at me with a softened gaze and nods.

"Anna, don't worry, I'm going to get better, and Nora is taking care of me."

Anna shakes her head, glares back out the window, and asks, "How did it happen between the two of you, Mother?"

"Are you sure you want to know the answers to your question, Anna?" She nods, so I begin: "From the minute Nora walked into my home, I knew how special she was. The week the two of you spent with me was wonderful, and I mean you too, Anna. Nora and I developed intimate feelings for one another during the week. I invited her back to Savannah the next day the two of you returned to Birmingham, and then she and I drove here to *Blowing Rock* together."

With a deep sigh she looks me in the eyes and asks, "Have the two of you slept together?"

Gazing at Anna, I softly say, "Anna, I'm in love with Nora, so yes, we have become intimate."

Anna seems very upset but is obviously holding it in due to my sickness. "Anna, you don't have to understand, but I love you and want you in my life." She glances back at me and begins to weep. "Anna, come here," I say softly.

After a moment, she lays her head against me and begins to cry as I hold her close. "Anna, you're my daughter, and I love you. I always have." Anna lifts her head and wipes her tears away.

She looks at me, lets out a deep sigh, and says, "Mother, I might be able to handle this better if it were with a woman closer to your own age. But my god, Nora is not only my friend but twenty-one years younger!" She glares at me, waiting for a response.

"Anna, before your father and I met, I was in love with a woman during my time in college. I loved her deeply, but our family expectations and society doomed our relationship. Those constraints no longer exist for me, and I don't care what others think at my age. I'm in love with Nora, and she is going to remain in my life." I gaze at her intently, then add, "I would love for you to be more a part of my life, Anna."

She looks at me and chuckles. "Well, I guess this is what Dad meant when he said you were not capable of loving him."

Beginning to cough again, I see Nora walking back through the door. She rushes to my side and sits beside me while Anna glares at her.

Nora

As the nurse enters to take Vanessa's vitals again, Anna walks out of the room, and I follow her. "Anna, wait," I call out. She stops and waits for me to catch up before looking at me.

"Let's go to the waiting area, Anna. No one was in there a

moment ago." She nods, and we make our way to the empty waiting room.

Anna sits down and sighs loudly, expressing her displeasure with our relationship. She stares straight ahead and says, "Well, I've known that you prefer women, Nora, but I had no idea my mother did." Then she lets out a light chuckle.

"I wish to God I'd never taken you home to Savannah with me," she says, anger lacing her words.

After a moment, I reply, "And the last thing I wanted to do at one o'clock this morning was call you, Anna, but I did. I'm sure our friendship is over, but your mother is an amazing woman. She's nothing like the person you described, and it's a damn shame you can't see that."

Turning to me, she says, "It won't last, Nora. Mother is simply replacing me with you, and you're obviously in need of a mother since yours is dead." Then she stands up and walks down the hall and out the front door.

As I watch the door close, I whisper under my breath, "You bitch," before quickly heading back into Vanessa's room. Upon entering, I see Vanessa's weak but warm smile.

"Come here, baby," she says sweetly. I pull her into my arms, holding her tightly. She looks up and asks, "Was she rude to you, Nora?"

"It doesn't matter, darling. What matters is that I'm in love with you. That's bigger than any opinions or rude remarks from others, even hers."

"My lovely Nora," she whispers as she lies back, closes her eyes, and drifts off gently.

CHAPTER 14

VANESSA

After three days in the hospital, I've made great progress and feel remarkably better. With a bit of persuasion, I was able to convince the doctor to let me leave, promising I would remain in bed.

Nora went to the cabin earlier to load up our luggage and other items and is returning to the hospital. Entering my room with a giggle, she says, "Well, hello Mrs Lord, you look scrumptious and yummy."

Laughing at her, I reply, "That's good because I feel so much better and am ready for you to feast on me, Nora Wolfe." Then she laughs as she takes me in her arms.

"Hmmm," I moan into her neck, kissing it as Vanessa chuckles at me.

Sitting beside me, Nora says, "I hate that we can't return to your Savannah home yet. I called some other photographers I trust to cover the wedding for me this weekend, but they all have other obligations."

"Nora, my love, it's quite alright. Besides, I'm looking forward to spending time with you in your apartment."

"My tiny apartment?" she asks, shaking her head.

Threading my fingers through her blonde hair, I reply, "Of course, Nora. Our home isn't in Savannah, love; it's wherever you and I are together."

Pulling away, Nora replies, "Yes, it is Vanessa. No wonder the cabin felt like home to me.

Nora and I are on our way back to Birmingham after they discharged me around mid-morning. Lying in the back seat under warm blankets, I comically say, "If you get tired of driving, love, I can take over."

Nora laughs loudly and replies, "Okay, darling. When I fill up with gas, we can switch places."

Snuggling against my pillow, I laugh softly, feeling safe and loved as I gaze at Nora. Watching her drive my car makes my heart swell with happiness. "I'm really looking forward to staying at your 'tiny apartment,' as you call it, baby. I've wondered what it looks like, and I bet it's exactly how I imagined you living."

Sitting up a bit, my eyes catch Nora's in the rearview mirror. I wink at her; she giggles and says, "You still have a way of unnerving me, Vanessa. I suppose I'll never get past being completely smitten by you."

"I hope not, Nora, because I am totally love-struck by you. As our eyes meet again in the mirror, I gaze at those Emerald Coast eyes of hers, knowing that she is my future—my home, my everything.

EPILOGUE ONE

VANESSA

May 1948
The Emerald Coast

"Two Mojito's coming up," I hear Nora say as I gaze up, meeting her eyes.

"Thank you, baby," I reply as I hold her eyes, then add, "We should make a toast. I know it's unusual to toast with Mojito's, but you and I obviously aren't rule followers, Miss Wolfe."

With a robust laugh, Nora replies, "Let's toast to Nietzsche and his ideals about individualism. He said, and I quote: 'Become who you are.'"

Clinking Nora's glass with mine, I gaze into her lovely face and say, "I've never been happier in my entire life than I am at this moment, sweetheart."

Nora takes a sip of her Mojito, stands, straddles me, and sits slowly in my lap. With a wide grin, I say, "You're a bad girl, Nora Wolfe, and I love that about you, baby." Then I laugh as I hold her close.

Nora stands again, turns around to gaze at the Gulf Coast, and then slowly lowers her seductive body down onto mine again. "Good god, Nora, I made it through pneumonia, but you're eventually going to give me heart failure with this young, sexy body of yours.

"One could only hope, Vanessa," she says as she laughs, pressing her back against my bosoms. Sitting my Mojito down, I grab her, pull her tightly against me, and laugh.

As our laughter subsides, I continue holding her, sipping my drink, and watching the waves crash effortlessly against the beach. "Look out at that sparkling blue-green water, Nora. I told you that your eyes were the color of the Emerald Coast."

Turning her head toward me, she says, "You told me that the day I returned from Birmingham, back to you, Vanessa." Then she pauses for a moment, "I'll never forget the look you gave me as I peered out the train window. At that moment, I knew I belonged to you, darling."

"Nora," I whisper, "I remember that moment so vividly, and it's precisely how I felt, too. I knew in that instant that you belonged to me, sweetheart."

Turning slightly toward me, Nora lays her head against my shoulder and lets me love her. "Do you think Anna will eventually come around?" She asks softly.

Threading my fingers through her hair as I gaze at the crashing waves, I reply, "I don't know, Nora. Maybe in time, but I'm happy and content regardless."

Nora sits up, takes a sip of her Mojoita, and then gazes at the water. "What's on your mind, Nora?" I ask, gripping soft strands of her blonde hair.

"Oh, something Anna said at the hospital."

Sitting up, I pull Nora close and ask, "What did she say to you?"

Shaking her head, she replies quietly, "Oh, something like: Our love won't last, that you're just replacing her with me, and that I need a mother because mine is dead."

Immediately I grow angry at Anna, but I close my eyes and remember how she is. Gently, I ask, "What is your opinion about that, Nora?"

Nora stands and sits facing me on the lounge chair, watching the waves. Then she replies, "For some reason, I've allowed that to eat at me, Vanessa."

Sitting up, I say, "Nora, you can't possibly believe that."

Glancing at me, she replies, "Perhaps I just need you to help me realize that it isn't true."

Taking her hand in mine, I say, "Look at me, Nora." As she raises her eyes, I ask, "What do you feel about me as a woman?"

Nora gazes at me and says, "That night in the motel room on our way to *Blowing Rock*, I told you that you're the most alluring woman I've ever known, Vanessa. And I still feel that way about you."

Interlacing her fingers in mine, I ask, "And what does alluring mean to you, Nora?"

With a grin and nod, she replies, "To me, It means attractive and seductive."

"Is that how you see me, Nora?"

With my hand against her cheek, she meets my eyes and whispers, "Yes, Vanessa, but I feel so many other things for you, too."

"As I do you, Nora. Then I say, "Hell, even if her statement is a tiny bit true, what in the hell would it matter, Nora."

She grins at me and says, "It doesn't matter, Vanessa. Thank you, darling."

"For what, Nora?"

"Thank you for acknowledging how I feel about that," she replies as she gazes into my eyes.

"Nora, I still see you as my young lover, as I've told you from the beginning, but I sure don't look at you like a daughter, baby. You can bet your sweet sexy ass I don't love."

Nora laughs loudly, then stands and walks to the back door of the beach house and says, "Do you remember that compromising position I told you I fantasized about the first night I met you?"

Nodding with a chuckle, I say, "Of course, love."

There's plenty of room on this couch. Grab that Mojita and follow me," she says seductively, then gives me a slow wink.

As I chase her inside, Nora says, "Sit, darling." With a grin, I take a seat on the sofa. Nora removes her clothing and asks, "Do you remember that morning in the cabin when I laid across you with nothing but my robe on?" Then she lays across my lap."

As I rub her ass, I say, "Oh yes, love. I remember that morning vividly.

Nora laughs and then says, "That made me incredibly wet and on the verge of an orgasm."

Rubbing her ass and then gripping her blonde hair, I seductively ask, "I believe I grabbed your hair as I rubbed your ass. Didn't I?

"Oh, Vanessa. Yes, it was exactly like this," She coos. Moving down her ass slowly, I find her warm wetness. Nora gasps.

"Does this feel good, baby?" I ask as I press softly against her clit.

"Yes, you have no idea how good this feels," Nora says breathlessly.

Pressing harder against her clit I whisper, "Tell me how it feels, Nora?"

She giggles softly and replies, "Like I'm helpless, and I can only submit to you."

"Hmmm, I like how that sounds, Nora," I say as I continue gripping her hair and pressing against her clit.

"I'm ready to come, darling, but don't let me just yet," she says, whimpering.

Gripping her hair tighter, I ease the pressure from her clit to hold her orgasm back for a moment. "You're going to come so good for me, baby. Aren't you, Nora,"

With a gasp, she replies, "Yes."

After fighting it for a few moments, Nora murmurs, "I can't hold back any longer, Vanessa." With a grin, I press harder against her clit, making firm circles as I keep her hair clutched in my hand.

"Come for me, Nora," I whisper. Immediately, Nora begins to orgasm. With a fistful of her flaxen blonde hair in my hand, I watch my young lover orgasm as she lies in my lap. 'Helpless,' as she said. Again and again, Nora orgasms as I watch my young woman submissive to my touch.

As the last orgasm ends, Nora relaxes, and her body falls weak. Releasing the grasp on her hair, I begin threading it through my fingers lovingly as I rub her ass softly. "You're mine, Nora. And you always will be, baby," I say tenderly.

"Vanessa, there could never be another woman for me," she says as she giggles.

EPILOGUE TWO

NORA

Savannah, Georgia
September 1, 1948

Holding Vanessa in my arms, I gaze at the two paintings on our bedroom wall and smile. She said that day at the summit of *Blowing Rock* that she would hang them on the wall of our bedroom once she painted them. Smiling at them, I think about how the last several months of my life have changed.

I moved in with Vanessa this past March after I completed all of my pending photography obligations. As soon as I got settled in, I began marketing my photography services here in Savannah.

Vanessa insisted that I take over the sunroom as my own space for photography. So now I shoot there occasionally, but I mainly use it to meet with clients and show my work.

"Good morning, love," she whispers.

Giggling, I say, "Well, good morning, darling. Did you sleep well?"

Vanessa begins to moan and growl at me as I laugh. "I'll take that as a yes, darling."

Grabbing me, she rolls over me and shouts, "Happy 30th Birthday, Nora Wolfe. You're finally out of your twenties!"

Finding some of my aggressive strength that she adores, I immediately roll her and, in a flash, am sitting on top of her, straddling her. "How in the hell do you always manage to do that to me, Nora?!" she exclaims.

"Because I'm your wildcat, remember," I say, then purr at her.

"You're right about that, love. You are indeed a damn wildcat," She says, then sits up and grabs me. "I have a million things planned for us today, so let's get up and shower."

Running my fingers through her hair, I grasp it and say, "It's my birthday, Miss Lord. Maybe I want to spend it with you all day in bed fucking."

"Oh god, Nora. You are indeed going to give me a heart attack," she says, then falls back against the bed.

Climbing off of her, I say, "Well, if you don't want to fuck me, then I'll go get in a shower." Grabbing me, she pulls me back to the bed and laughs.

"Come here, Nora, you silly wicked girl. I have your first birthday gift for you," she says sweetly as she opens the drawer on her nightstand and pulls out a small box.

Sitting beside her, I gaze at her and smile. "You have the most beautiful smile, Nora. I'm so thankful for you," she says sweetly. Then she places the gift-wrapped box in my hand, kisses me, and says, "Happy birthday, my lovely Nora."

"What is it, Vanessa?" I ask with excitement.

"Open it, Nora," she says with a charming grin. Removing the gift wrap, I slowly open the box. Inside is a solitaire diamond ring on a gold band. I close my eyes and the box and hold it.

Touching my back, Vanessa asks, "Are you okay, Nora?"

As I nod, I lean against her. Vanessa takes me in her arms and says, "I love you, Nora. I've loved you since the day we met, baby."

"I know," I whisper softly, then add, "I've told you that you sometimes overwhelm me, Vanessa. This is one of those moments."

As Vanessa holds me, I feel her immense love enveloping me. "I love it when you allow me to see your vulnerability," she says softly.

"What does the ring mean? I know you love me, but why did you buy me a ring?" I ask, meeting her gaze. Vanessa smiles and tucks a piece of my hair behind my ear.

She caresses my face and replies, "Well, Nora, we've lived together since March, but you've been mine since last Christmas. Wouldn't you agree?"

"Yes, I most definitely have been," I say with a grin.

Vanessa takes the box from my hand, opens it, and removes the ring. She gazes at me, her smile radiant, then takes my left hand and slips the ring onto my ring finger. "Nora, this ring means I'm committed to you. I would be with or without it, but you're my beautiful young woman, Nora Wolfe, and I'm deeply and unconditionally in love with you."

Perhaps the ring is for both of us because the immense joy I feel as I glance at it on you makes me incredibly proud that you are mine, Nora."

Gazing at the beautiful ring, I smile, then glance up, meeting Vanessa's sweet brown eyes, and quietly say, "I feel like we're married, Vanessa."

With a wide grin, Vanessa pulls me close, kisses my lips tenderly, and softly says, "We are, Nora. That's what this ring means to me. Is that okay?"

Looking into her loving eyes, I see the woman I know without a doubt my loving parents sent me to last Christmas. "Yes, it's more than just okay, Vanessa, and I'm so in love with you," I reply with a grin. Then I add, "This perfect diamond symbolizes our lasting bond now and throughout eternity, darling."

THANK YOU

Thank you for reading *Romancing Miss Fitzgerald*. I hope you enjoyed it!
I'd love it if you would take a moment to leave a review on Amazon and share your thoughts. Your feedback would mean so much to me!

Aven

Facebook Aven Blair
TikTok @AvenBlairAuthor

ALSO BY AVEN BLAIR

Claire's Young Flame

Julian's Lady Luck

Evan's Entanglement

My Sapphires only Dance for Her

Driving Miss Kennedy

Sailing Mrs Clarkson

Escorting Miss Mercer

Flying Miss Lomax

Romancing Miss Fitzgerald

ABOUT THE AUTHOR

 Aven is a devoted author of age-gap sapphic lesbian romances, celebrated for her sweet yet fiery love stories that always promise a happily ever after. Writing from her quaint Southern town, she crafts captivating narratives centered around strong Southern women as they navigate love and life in historical settings. With a blend of warmth, humor, and emotional depth, Aven's stories enchant readers with unforgettable romances and her unwavering commitment to love in all its forms.